A Winter Seige

Elvish Chronicles, Volume 3

Prudence MacLeod

Published by Prudence MacLeod, 2024.

A Winter Siege
Third Chronicle in the tale of the Elves of Elandor
(second edition)
by
Prudence MacLeod
Copyright April 22 / 2017

A WINTER SEIGE

First edition. March 19, 2024.

ISBN: 978-1927478776

Written by Prudence MacLeod.

In the Spring that followed the year of rescue, the Elves came boiling out of the north, driving all before them. The peoples of Elandor fled the villages and farms to seek refuge in the cities, there to hide behind stone walls for protection from the freed slaves and the ancient Borni warriors. A standoff was reached, and then the snows of winter began to fall.

In this, the third Chronicle of the Elves of Elandor, I shall relate some of the hardships and victories of that long and bitter winter.

Snowfall

The village of Argar had grown to the size of a town as the Elves brought more and more people there. Lord Tanis used a table at the inn for his headquarters as he conducted the dual sieges of the Geni ruled cities. Both Magdan and the capital city of Shotar were overrun with refugees and besieged by the elusive Elves.

Despite these successes, the young Elvish commander didn't lower his guard, but remained focused. He sat musing softly as he and the mage mulled over the logistics. "So, Eline is taking Ethor and a hundred new Bornani into the mountains to winter at the way stations?"

"Yes, my Lord Tanis. The queen and her lady companion reside at Fugitive now, but with all the new Orcs and Bornani, Fugitive couldn't hold them all. You're concerned?"

"I am, Trelanth, could you take a look and see if Eline made it through before this storm hit?" The mage nodded her head then settled into a meditation. No one disturbed her.

HIGH IN THE MOUNTAINS above the town of Fugitive, two Elves on watch stood beside a tall boulder, nearly invisible to anyone on the trail. They and their companions had worked feverishly through the summer to get the way station ready for the Bornani to use as a rest stop on their long journey north to Elfhone. Now the work was done, and winter was setting in. "What a delightful winter's day! I think something interesting will happen today."

"You sure about that?" grinned his companion. "It rarely ever does."

He winked at her mischievously. "Count on it."

"What would be truly interesting is if that bank of cloud would turn away," she said.

His mood sobered. "Aye, that's the truth of it, but we have another problem. Look coming." There was a dark line of moving figures slowly climbing through the pass. "I wonder, are they friend or foe?"

"I'll go ask them," she chuckled as she stepped out from behind her boulder.

"You be careful, Del."

"I will. If they're unfriendly I'll lead them into the blind canyon. You'll have to drop me a rope to get me out."

"Got it right here." He grinned as she trotted away towards the oncoming mass of people. Del soon recognized the queen's banner, and with a shout of glee, leaped towards them. Within moments she was on her way back at a full run. She didn't even pause as she passed him. "Come on, we've got work to do."

He followed closely as she raced away, heading for the way station.

It was quite late in the year for newly freed Bornani to be making the trek across the mountains. "Get the fires up," he shouted as they neared the station. Several Elves set to work building up fires along the sheltered valley.

Back on the trail, Eline sighed with delight as the land began to level off then slope downwards. In the distance she could see the smoke of many fires rising out of a forested valley. The only thing that could dampen her spirits now was the heavy cloud bank moving swiftly across the sky. She hoped they'd make it to the way station before the storm hit.

At her shout the Elves broke into a run. The land sloped downward and there were trees ahead. The first flakes of snow were dancing in the air as they passed through the trees and found the large encampment beside the stream.

As they neared Eline saw a short, but stout wall surrounded a well spread out grouping of buildings. Fires were dancing in the open spaces and also in some of the shelters. There were three long storehouses and a makeshift forge.

The garrison had been busy, and the storehouses proved to be full. If necessary, the entire group could pass the winter there. They'd have to hunt and forage a bit, but the valley was long and well forested. They would have shelter and food.

The gates were open, and the Elves poured through, spreading out to warm themselves by the fires. As the last one passed the gate ten warriors trotted out into the storm. "Where are they going?" asked Eline.

"Masking your trail," replied Del as she approached Eline and Ethor. "By nightfall your trail will end at the summit. So, Eline, what do you think?"

"I'm amazed. You few have built an entire village in the course of a summer."

"We've worked hard, that's for sure. The idea was to build an empty village, one easily defended, yet one that could be abandoned if need be. There's enough room here for you to spend the winter, and we shouldn't have to do a lot of foraging. It'll be good to have some company."

"Del, we're not all staying. We'll leave about fifty Bornani with you and take the rest on to Station One."

"So, you'll winter there?"

"No, once we drop them off, we'll be coming back through to Fugitive."

"No you won't," replied Del as she looked upwards into the storm. "If this is going to be as bad as I expect, the high pass will be blocked until spring."

"Seriously?"

"Eline, believe me. Look, we've never spent a winter here, but old Vigo has."

"Who's old Vigo?"

"Early the past summer, a small family of Dwarves wandered in, looking to trade and to see what we were up to. He asked if we needed a smith and we readily agreed. He tends the forge and the other three of them tend the storehouses. Auggie is an awesome cook. If she weren't already bonded to Viggo, I might ask her myself."

"I heard that," rumbled a deep voice as a Dwarf couple approached. The woman was chuckling, and he was shaking a finger at Del. "You can just forget about stealing my cook, Elf."

Del introduced them. "Del tells me this storm will block the pass, Viggo, is that right?"

"It is. We've been in this valley for a long time, and I'm actually surprised you made it through. That pass will be blocked until spring now. There's a few deep caverns further down the valley where you could retreat to if the snows get too deep, but otherwise I'd stay clear."

"Oh? Why?"

"Something evil dwells deep in those caverns. Tall and ugly, they are, and hard to kill. You have enough warriors, you'd most likely be able to drive them off, but we couldn't. We left, came out in the open, but most of the clan stayed back to fight."

"So what happened to them?" asked Ethor.

"No idea," he sighed. "It's been a few years now and none of them have ever come out. So, Del tells me there are Dwarves in Fugitive, is that right?"

"Yes, it's true. There's a small clan there now."

"Aye then, perhaps we'll take a trip down there for a visit come summer."

"You'd be welcomed in Fugitive," smiled Eline. "Now, before we start next summer's visiting, tell me what we should do to survive the winter. I'd like to take half our people on to the next way station. What do you think my chances are?"

"Not good, girl. You'd be fine traveling down the valley, but you'd have one more high pass to cross. I expect this storm will block that one too."

"So, we're stuck here for the winter?"

"Aye, it'll be good to have some company, someone to keep Del occupied and out of trouble."

SLOWLY TRELANTH SHOOK off the spell. It had been difficult to see over that distance through the storm. "All is well, my Lord. Eline has reached the first way station, but I fear she'll go no further before the spring comes to the mountains. This storm is a bad one, and it'll block the passes through the peaks."

"But they're safe there, they'll survive the winter?"

"Have no fear, Tanis my friend, Eline has survived and thrived through worse than this."

He sighed and nodded his head. "Then I'm content."

"Tanis, the Spirit Pull isn't the only way we Elves choose a mate, in point of fact, it rarely is. If your heart calls for Eline, perhaps you should speak of it to her?"

Another gentle shake of the head. "No, Trelanth. I'll not speak of this only to have her snatched away to another by the Compulsion two or three years from now."

Wisely, she said nothing more, simply rose and patted his shoulder as she left the room.

At the Walls of Shotar

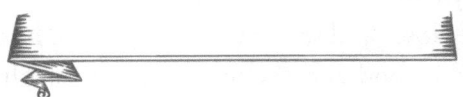

In the Geni city of Shotar the people huddled against the cold and hunger. The king had sent a number of hunters out through the gates to fetch meat, but none ever returned. The Elves held the forests, none who entered ever survived.

Outside the gates of the city the refugees who couldn't gain entry to the city huddled against the high walls, out of the wind. Little food was parceled out from within the city, and what was given was instantly claimed by the strong who had forced the elders and the weak further from the walls. What food those people received was delivered by the Elves of the forest, but now the snows had begun, and game was becoming scarce.

Kern the Horseman, with his bonded companion Dera close at his side, had led a successful campaign against the city of Shotar. No hunter from the city survived. The men at arms who escorted the slaves out to gather and glean food from the abandoned farms nearby fell to the wild horsemen and the slaves were set free. Shotar had received no supplies from that quarter either, and now snow was falling.

"Kern, my beloved, is this wise?"

"Not by half," chuckled the young Elf as he took his companion by the hand and led her through the falling snow. His lame leg was a hindrance when on the ground at the best of times, but in deepening snows, movement was a major struggle. Ah well, there was no help for it.

A few moments later they reached the wall and the large numbers of humans and orcs huddled there out of the howling winds. These were the people pushed furthest from the gates, the old, infirm, and the youngest without adults. Dera stepped closer and wrapped the old Orc female in a heavy cloak.

Kern leaned closer and spoke to her above the howling wind. "Go with Dera, there is food and shelter nearby." Struggling, the old Orc followed Dera who took her by the hand and led her through the storm.

Another Elf stepped up to Dera's place and passed a cloak to the next person, a small Orc child, it was unable to stand on its own. The Elf scooped the child into his arms and followed Dera. Still another Elf stepped up. This time it was an old human woman. A dozen in all were taken away before the supplies ran out and Kern painfully forced his way through the snow toward the waiting trees.

Suddenly a huge shape appeared from the swirling snow and he shouted with glee as he leaped to the horse's back. In mere moments he was in the forest and soon reached the small camp. There, beneath a large stand of tall trees were a dozen Elves, tending the refugees by the fire, warming them, bringing them food.

As he dismounted and lightly kissed Dera's cheek, an old Orc rose to face him. "You're the war leader here?"

"I am. I see you're warming up nicely."

"Yes, I am that. I owe you, war leader. I'm old and infirm with age, but I can still fight. I'll need weapons."

"No need for that, my friend. Sit, eat, warm your bones by the fire, for that's what I intend to do."

The Orc chuckled and gratefully sat back down. "This cloak has the king's insignia on it, and blood stains as well. I assume the original owner had no further use for it."

Kern laughed as he threw his cloak around Dera's shoulders and snuggled her close. "No, my friend, he doesn't. The king sends men out of the city to hunt and gather. Those who enter the forest don't return. We take the cloaks, boots, weapons, and food rations. We give it to those pushed furthest from the gates."

"Why? I'm pleased that you do, but can't imagine why you would do that."

"I was a slave, a boy, lame and useless. Master sent me to the killing sheds. He planned to buy a new slave at the auctions. Queen Ariel sacked the city and brought us all out. She brought us to the Borni who taught us how to be true Elves.

"During that journey I asked the queen to kill me so I wouldn't slow the others down, be a burden to them. She refused and made me her horseman. From there I rose to become second to Lord Tanis, commander of a thousand warriors. The lesson here, my friend, is this. As long as you draw breath, you can be useful. If I let you starve or freeze to death, I gain nothing."

"Keep me alive and you gain a burden, it's a hard truth, but a truth, nonetheless."

"Ha, forget that, brother. You'll have to earn your keep."

"Name the task, war leader, and I'll do it or die trying."

"First, you warm up a bit, then we rest until the storm passes. Two days travel from here we have a farm wagon and two draft horses to pull it. Can you drive such a wagon, handle the horses?"

"I was a farmer most of my life, I believe I can still manage that. What am I hauling in the wagon?"

"All these people, a few sacks of food, and some farm tools. We scavenged it all from the farms we burned out. Two days further on is another wagon, loaded with root vegetables and corn. There is a town called Argar, do you know it?"

"I do."

"Go there, deliver the wagon and the people to the headman, a woman named Grace. My commander, Lord Tanis will be there. Tell him all is well at the walls of Shotar, and that you have to return for the second wagon. He'll help you."

The old Orc nodded. "I'll do all in my power to deliver your wagons, but what happens then?"

"My friend, you'll be welcome in Argar, I swear it. The people there will care for you and your cargo. Lord Tanis may find uses for a hard working farmer at that. As I said before, if you still draw breath you can be useful."

"So, I assume your folk will remain here, watching the gates."

"Of course, you know, in case the king decides to donate any more supplies for his people who remain outside the walls."

The old Orc chuckled at that. "So, tell me, why did you burn us out and steal our food and farms in the first place?"

"We needed to fill Shotar with refugees."

"To use up all their food supplies over the winter. Starving warriors are less effective than well fed ones. Makes sense to me. Are you certain Argar has a place for us?"

"If not I'll take you to Fugitive. The Orcs there will take you in if I ask them."

"You'd do that? Why?"

"The chieftain of the Scratite Clan lives there. The man is a fierce warrior and a close ally of the queen. If I learned anything from him it's the meaning of honor and its importance. We swore as we burned out the farms that we'd do all in our power to help the people we had to displace. It's the only honorable thing to do."

The Orc laughed and slapped Kern on the shoulder. "Boy, lame or not, you'd make a fine Orc. I give you my word of honor I'll do what you ask or die in the attempt."

Kern grinned. "Thank you, my friend. You won't travel alone in the forest. Always near if needed, will be a number of warriors, watching out for you."

"You don't suppose they might leave a bit of meat by the wagon from time to time, would they?"

That made Kern laugh. "You never know, they just might."

A while later Dera finished feeding the last child then wrapped him in a warm cloak. Patting his shoulder and telling him to stay by the fire, she rose and sought out Kern. "You're troubled, my love, I can feel it. What disturbs you so?"

"The storm, Dera. If this continues for long the snows will be too deep for the horses. We have to find some place for them to pass the winter, a place where they can find food."

"You spoke of such a place before."

"That's in Narthwood, well beyond our reach now."

"What can we do?"

"At the town of Argar there are broad open fields, the winds should keep them clear enough, and there is fodder in the barns. They'll be fine there."

"So, we go back?"

"We do." He sighed and his shoulders slumped.

"Kern, what is it?"

"Dera, if we leave, many of those beside the walls will die before the coming of spring. They'll die of the cold, of hunger, and disease."

"Kern, we can't save them all, you know this."

"I know, but there's the matter of hunters from within the walls as well. It's our task to prevent them from succeeding. How can we do that if we abandon this place?"

"Then the Reavers won't abandon it. We leave them here to complete the task while you and I take the horses to Argar."

He turned and gave her a hard look, but she just smiled and gently squeezed his shoulder. "Kern, it's not your *warrior of the forest* skills that caused Lord Tanis to make you his second, it's your wisdom, your insights. My love, you know you can't run through the deep snows like the others, you need a horse under you."

His shoulders slumped as he admitted the truth of her words. Only then did he notice another Elf standing near, waiting for a chance to speak. "Lora?"

"Dera has the right of it, Kern. She's spoken the words I had for you. Understand this, I've served under no more able leader than you, but the deep snow is the weakness in your armor. Kern, like Lord Tanis, you've kept us all informed of the desired tactics at every turn. Leave us here, we'll do this for you."

"So, have you already chosen my replacement as leader?"

"Kern ..."

"Forgive me, Lora, that was unkind and undeserved. I'm just bitter that I have to abandon my post."

The woman stepped closer and gripped his shoulder. "Hear me well, Kern the Horseman. You're not abandoning your post. You're the horseman, and we need those horses. These beautiful animals gave us many victories we couldn't have achieved without them. We need them, and you're the one they look to, you and you alone can get them to safety.

"Kern, there will be only one or two hunters come this winter, if any do. The Reavers will remain here, feed the refugees as best we can, but that's the easy task at this point. Getting the horses to safety, keeping them alive through the winter, that's by far the more challenging task right now, and you're the only man with any real chance of success. You know this to be true."

Kern nodded and accepted his fate. "As much as it galls me, I can see the sense in this. If I remain I'll be little more than a burden. At least, with the horses I can do something useful. All right, let's call them in and get this settled."

As Kern limped back toward the fires he didn't see Dera reach out to lightly grip Lora's shoulder and mouth the words, "Thank you." Lora grinned and winked at her then followed them back.

When all his troops were gathered, Kern spoke. "The snows grow deeper, and Dera has joined forces with Lora to forbid me from running through the drifts all winter." There was a round of chuckles at that.

"People, the horses need to get to more open lands where they can forage. The snows will be too deep here in the forests of Shotar. So, I'm being banished back to Argar. However, we have a mission here, and I'm loathe to abandon it. Since Lora has been so mean to me, I'm leaving her in charge." Another round of laughter followed that.

"I need a dozen warriors to come with me. We'll take these good folk who joined us this day, pick up the wagon, and return to Agar. Tell me, are there any of the Bornani who worked the farms here?"

"You know there are, Kern," grinned one man as he stepped forward. "Shall we go with you to Argar so we can help with the planting in spring?"

"That was my thought. The Borni are well accustomed to running about in the woods all winter. We'll leave them here to plague Shotar. We leave at first light." The storm was still blowing hard and so they waited an extra day before leaving. The sun was shining on a winter wonderland as they set out, the horses slowly picking their way through and around the drifts.

Winters Are For Making Plans

While Kern headed out on his quest to get his beloved horses to a place where they could survive the winter, Queen Ariel and her companion, the ageless assassin Mearith the Merciless, rested in the town of Fugitive. This was the one place in all the world where Ariel fully relaxed, felt at home. Here she spent her days with close friends, but a winter's adventure was approaching in the footsteps of a huge Orc.

"That was a storm worth remembering," muttered Drakkat, Chieftain of the Scratite Clan, as he stomped the snow from his boots. It had taken him a while to fight his way from his hut to the inn. Ariel and Mearith were enjoying a hot breakfast of oatmeal as he entered.

"Ho, Chieftain," grinned Mearith. "Have you broken your fast yet, or just the snow drifts from here to Shotar?"

"I could eat." He made for their table as Ariel indicated he should join them.

"What's on your mind, my brother in arms?" asked Ariel.

"Peace and quiet," he grumbled. "Saggit has moved himself, his new mate, and her children into my house, and there's not a minute's peace to be had. The girl child clings to my leg like a leech and the boy spends his time telling me how he plans to avenge his father. If I'd known my fate before I fought him I'd have let him win."

This brought a round of hearty laughter from all in the room. "Perhaps I have a solution," grinned Ariel.

"My queen, I can see the mischief in your eyes. What are you planning to do to me?"

"Drakkat, as I understand Orc society, the chieftain's mate holds great status, and she commands a lot of respect and obedience. Am I right?"

"Yes, that's the way of it."

"The problem here is you have no mate to defend you. Since Saggit is your brother, his companion is taking over the responsibilities of Chieftain's mate, yes?"

"Again, you have the right of it."

"So, I suggest you choose a mate." That brought a round of snickers and guffaws from the assembled folk, but they were startled at his response.

"That's the plan. I came this morning to tell you I'm leaving for the walls of Shotar to find a mate."

"Drakkat?"

"My queen, the snows are deep, and nothing of note will pass here for months. We emptied a lot of saddles here when we were attacked by the warriors of Shotar. The families those warriors who didn't return will all be outside the walls of Shotar now, struggling to stay alive. I'll have little trouble finding a mate there."

"So, you'll just march up to the most likely woman and take her away?" asked Ariel.

"Yes."

"All right, talk to me, my old friend."

"Orcs aren't Elves, Lady Ariel. We don't mate because some unknown god force locks us together, nor do we breed like rabbits with all and sundry as the humans do. Yes, we do love, and love powerfully, but it grows with time.

"Lady, Orcs endure, we survive. We work together and survive. Saggit chose the mate of a fallen chieftain, a man I killed in battle, yet she dotes on him as he does her. Together they'll work to make the clan stronger, more prosperous."

"By taking over your job?" grinned Marc.

"Ha, I know what they're doing," replied Drakkat. "They've decided I need a mate, and so they're trying to drive me to it. Sadly, it's working all too well. If I'm to have any peace at all this winter I must take a mate to shut them up." This brought another round of laughter.

"So, you're off to the walls of Shotar. Want some company for the journey?" asked Ariel.

"My queen?"

"Mearith and I will be running about in the forest all winter anyway. We have people scattered all across the land. In truth we're spread out a lot thinner than I'd like. We plan to check in with them all, so we might as well start with Shotar."

"You've been plotting with Saggit, haven't you?" said Drakkat. "Now you're planning to take an escort to make sure I follow through and not just run away."

"Why Drakkat, perish the thought. I know full well you'd never run away from a battle."

There was another round of laughter at that. Drakkat let his massive shoulder slump. "You're heartless, Lady Ariel. You've been with that Borni assassin too long." Mearith grinned and punched him lightly on the arm.

Drakkat grinned as well and shook his head. "All right then, when do we leave?"

"How about now?" Ariel laughed as she jumped to her feet. "Mearith's been cooped up inside walls too long and she's getting restless for the forests."

"Actually, I am," said Mearith as she rose from the table. "I'll put together a couple of packs while you make sure Drakkat doesn't escape."

"And I'll send Korath and the guard ahead to meet us at the walls of Magdan."

Saggit and his mate Kreen, stood side by side watching Drakkat and the two Elves enter the forest on the far side of the field. "Well, there he goes," grinned Saggit.

"That took long enough, can we go home now?"

"Yes, my girl, we can return to our own house now. Tired of being the chieftain's mate?"

"It's not my place, and everybody knows that. Once he brings her home she can take over and I can go back to being a mate and mother. I'll help her all I can if she'll let me, Saggit, you know this, but it's not my place, nor do I want it."

He grinned as he hugged her shoulders. "Let's tidy the place up for them now, and then go home. The house is buried in snow, I can see it from here."

THEY STOOD JUST INSIDE the trees, their breath rising in steamy clouds. "Mearith, what have we done, what misery have we wrought?"

"Easy, Ariel, my delight, easy. There was no choice, we did what we had to do."

"But, there must be over a thousand of them, Mearith, and I can see dead bodies from here. The scent of death is drawing the wolves. This will bring more death. These people aren't the Geni, they're innocents."

"Innocents, Ariel? How many of them put the whip to an Elf's back? How many ate their fill while the Elf who prepared the meal starved on a bowl of oshar a day?"

"I know, my love, I know. It's just..."

"Your soft loving heart cries out to feed them, I know. Ariel, the snows are too deep now or perhaps we could ... Look there, what do you see?"

Both Ariel and Drakkat squinted against the glare of the sun on the snow. What they saw made Drakkat chuckle. It was a couple of Elves, staying tight to the walls while they slipped into the camp of refugees, carrying the carcass of a deer. They dropped it beside the fire then faded back towards the forest while the hungry refugees quickly skinned the deer then began cooking the meat.

"Well now," smiled Ariel. "I believe I'd like to go have a chat with those Elves. You're on your own now, Drakkat. I expect to be introduced to a new sister when I return to Fugitive."

"Then I'd best be about the task." He shouldered his axe and began wading through the drifts towards the refugee camp, staying well out of sight of the guards high up on the walls. Mearith and Ariel moved back into the trees then circled around the city, seeking out the Elves they'd seen.

While Ariel and Mearith sped through the forest, a huge Orc approached the refugee camp. "Stay back," hissed an old woman, "there's no food here. You look strong enough. Go bang on the gates, they'll take you in and feed you if you swing that axe for them."

"Peace, woman," came that deep rumbling voice. "Eat this, it will give you strength." He passed her a small cake of pressed berries and mashed roots.

She snatched it from his hand and devoured it. "Is there more?" Others had drawn closer now.

"That was the last. Now, I want something in return."

Suddenly wary she took a step further away from him. "What do you want?"

"I see that this camp is mostly humans. I seek the camp of the Orcs."

"That way," said a man, his hand trembling as he pointed the way. "Beware the gates. If they see you ..."

"Understood."

Drakkat moved closer to the gates then stopped just out of sight. He could see the Orc's encampment and sank to the ground to wait, his heart heavy at what he was seeing. The Orcs had managed to push most of the humans farther away from the gates from which the food might come, but it was also obvious that little or no food came past that forbidding barrier.

Within that camp the stronger had pushed the weaker further away. There were several dead bodies lying in the snows to attest to the hardships the elderly and infirm faced.

It was close to high sun when Drakkat spotted her. An Orc female with a small child tended carefully to an elder at the outer edges of the camp. She left the child with the old man and moved into the camp, approaching the fire. Several tried to block her way, but her flashing daggers spoke of death or worse. They let her through.

She dipped her bowl in the cooking pot then returned to pass the bowl to the old man who shook his head and handed it to the child. When the bowl was empty she returned, but this time several makeshift spears barred her way. She was angry, threatening, but also weak from hunger and couldn't fight so many. She returned to huddle in their one large cloak with the man and the child.

As the sun fell behind the great walls she tried for the fire and cooking pot again, but failed. Those with spears blocked her path. "Stay back, Rakka, or we'll kill you and eat you from that pot. Your mate is dead, you have no status, no one to help you. Your whole clan is dead, get back into the snows and join them."

She cursed them soundly and stepped back, still facing them. Defeated, she turned to find a huge shape sitting beside her father and daughter. They were both eating something. As she stepped toward them, daggers at the ready, he rose and opened his cloak, exposing himself to her blades. Her eyes flew wide as the child stepped into that cloak and fished out another cake to eat from the pouch on his belt.

"Who are you? What do you want?"

"I'll tell you," he said as he swept off the cloak and wrapped it around her father's shoulders. "My name is Drakkat. I'm chieftain of the Scratite clan, allies of the Elf Queen. My clan is strong and well fed. I'll take you there if you'd like."

She lowered her daggers, but eyed him suspiciously. "At what cost?"

"If you go there you will face a lifetime of hard struggle," he chuckled. She just eyed him and gave him the look. "I came seeking a mate. I watched the people in the camp, but only in you did I see the strength and honor of a true Orc, a woman worthy to be the chieftain's mate."

She gazed at him for a long while, trying to figure out what he was up to. "Upon my honor and that of my clan, I swear I speak truth, woman. I offer myself and my clan to you, but your task will not be an easy one."

The child crawled into his arms, and he tucked her deeper into that cloak with her grandfather. A slow sad smile began to cross her face. "Here, eat this, it'll grant you strength." He passed her a cake of pressed berries, and with hands that trembled with hunger and the cold, she accepted and ate it.

She sighed with delight as she tasted the cake. While she ate he produced another cloak from his pack and stood up. She leaped back and drew her daggers. "It's made of wool, by the Elves. It'll warm you."

Others had noticed them and began to move closer, but he stepped past her, that huge axe leaping to his hand. "Stay back or meet your doom," he rumbled. "Make another move this way and I'll litter these snows with the blood of fools and cowards." They shrank away from this savage warrior, and he grunted in derision. "Vermin."

He turned back to her. "Why me, why not one of your own clan?" she asked.

"I need a woman fierce enough to defeat my brother's mate," he grinned. She quirked an eyebrow at him. "She's taken on the role of chieftain's mate, but doesn't want it, I can tell. They moved into my house and drove me nearly unto madness hoping I'd take a mate so she could pass off the task. Sadly, it worked."

"You don't really want a mate?"

"I didn't say that. Truth is, I didn't, until I saw you take food and bring it to an elder and child, not for yourself. You're weak from hunger and cold, yet you retain your honor. You're fierce enough to stand beside me in battle, and you're strong enough to help me make a true clan of the odds and ends of people we've adopted.

"Girl, we're Orcs, we don't find our mates like the humans, nor are we thrust together by the gods like the Elves, we're Orcs. We endure, we survive. We choose our mates to help us do that. Come with me, woman. Join with me against the Geni, help me make the Scratite strong."

She still hesitated, afraid to trust, eyeing him closely, trying to find the betrayal in his eyes, but finding none. He took the hand that held her dagger and pulled her gently closer. Raising that blade, he lightly cut his wrist, producing a few drops of blood, then released her. "So, what will it be, Rakka, will you remain here cowering beneath Geni walls, or will you join with me and face them in battle?"

Her eyes were wide now. "You offer a blood bond with me?"

"I do."

She hesitated for a moment longer then nodded. She nicked her own wrist then pressed her arm to his, rubbing the wounds together. "So be it, Drakkat of the Scratite, I'm yours now. I, my daughter, and my sire are all that's left of my clan. Do with us as you will."

Drakkat pulled her close and gave her a gentle hug. "Come, my mate. Let's be away from these accursed walls."

As he released her and turned the old man rose and opened the cloak, exposing his chest to the blow. "The snows are deep, and my days have been long. Make the blow swift. You can carry the child easily, there's no need to harm her."

"Nor will I," rumbled Drakkat. "But you're not getting off that easy. It's a long way to Fugitive and I'll need help to defend my family." He pressed a long dagger into the man's hand. "Keep this close. Who knows when you'll need it."

The old Orc was dumbfounded. "You're not going to kill me?"

Drakkat just grinned at him. "You're not that lucky, my friend. Queen Ariel says that if you can still draw breath you can be useful. You're still breathing, so I have work for you. Come family, darkness has fallen, and I want to be away from these walls before the light of day returns.

"Rakka, toss the young one onto my shoulders and I'll break trail through the snows. You and this warrior will defend my back. Let's go."

She smiled and shook her head as she followed the huge form across the snow in the moonlight. There was no danger, and he knew it. No one from the refugee camp would dare threaten this massive warrior. She doubted there was a warrior inside Shotar who would dare to face him. The walking was actually easier than she imagined it would be, for he took pains to trample down a path for her and her sire to follow.

It was near dawn when Rakka looked back to see two Elves masking their tracks through the snow. They were near the trees; she could smell food cooking and hear the crackle of a fire. Drakkat headed right toward it. Her eyes widened as she saw several Elves gathered around that fire. One woman stood to greet them and Drakkat knelt before her.

"Well, it's about time you got here. I was starting to think you couldn't find a suitable bride," she grinned impishly as she took the child from his shoulders and raised him up.

"What, did you expect me to choose the first female I saw? I was waiting for the best, the most beautiful and fiercest Orc woman alive."

"And I see that you found her," smiled Ariel. "Introduce us, if you please."

Grinning, Drakkat turned and gently pulled Rakka forward. "This woman is Rakka, my chosen mate. We are joined by a blood bond. Rakka, my bride, this woman is Lady Ariel, Queen of the Elves, and this woman is Mearith the Merciless, her bonded companion."

Rakka swallowed hard and sank to one knee as Drakkat had done. "Rise, Rakka of the Scratite, mate of my friend and brother in arms, Drakkat," smiled Ariel. "We will become great friends, you and I. Come, sit to the fire, rest, eat. The Elves will make certain you're not disturbed this day."

She rose and stepped away, signaling for another of the Elves. "Are you on your way, my queen?"

"Yes, Lora. I want to catch Kern as quickly as possible. Keep Drakkat and his people here for a couple of days, let them rest and feed them well. When they set out, make sure they have all they need for the journey back to Fugitive."

"It shall be as you desire, my queen." With that, Ariel and Mearith disappeared into the trees.

Rakka was gazing at the place where they vanished, and Drakkat was grinning at her. "Well?"

She slowly shook off the spell. "In truth, I thought you were ..."

"Lying through my teeth?"

"Yes, that. Why would a personal friend of the Elf Queen be at the walls of Shotar asking me to mate with him?"

"He was there because that's where the perfect mate for him was. Sadly, couldn't find her, so he chose another instead."

She spun to face him and saw the teasing grin on his face. She hit him on the shoulder, a blow that would have felled a lesser man, but he just laughed and hugged her close. "You'll pay for that one," she admonished.

"I have no doubt at all," he grinned as she snuggled into his arms. Perhaps it would all work out for the best. At least there was plenty of food now, and he'd brought her child and sire out as well. She decided to trust him to protect her, and she silently vowed to do all in her power to help him. As he'd said, together they'd survive and thrive.

Several days later they were deep in the forest, taking their time as they made their way toward Fugitive. Rakka knew he was taking his time to make it easy for the old man and the child to keep up. The food was starting to run low and Drakkat was about to settle them into a camp then go hunting. It wasn't necessary.

Drakkat was looking for a likely spot for a camp when he heard the horses ahead on the trail. They slipped behind a fallen tree, but he recognized the lone rider. He stepped out from behind the stump and called out. "What in the name of the gods would a blacksmith be doing on a horse in the middle of the forest at mid-winter?"

The Elf rider laughed as she leaped from the back of the beast and lit lightly in the snow. "Looking for a lost Orc," she replied. She stepped up and gripped his arm in the warrior's grip. "Well met, my friend. Was your quest successful?"

"It was." He grinned as he pulled Rakka forward. "Rakka, my bride, this woman is Lady Freida, sister to the queen."

"She of the magic sword?" Rakka breathed softly, then lowered her eyes and blushed.

"The same. So, you are Rakka, mate of Drakkat?"

"Yes, Lady."

"She looks strong, my friend. You should have an interesting life."

"I have no doubts," grinned Drakkat. "Lady Blacksmith, why have you come?"

"Others wanted to, especially Saggit and Marc, but they're needed for defense, as are you."

"Defense? Is Fugitive under attack?"

"Not as such, at least, not when I left. No, it's something else. Do you recall Ariel speaking of monsters, wolf hybrids that attacked her people on the road to Elfhome?"

"I do."

"They've been seen in the forests. We've lost two scouts to them, but they were fought off. They came again in the night and your clan took the brunt of that one. The Orcs drove them off, but everyone's on alert. It was agreed that you needed to be warned. It was also agreed that I was the most likely to survive alone in the forest.

"I have extra food and cloaks as well as weapons on the horses. The snows are deep, so I brought the tallest horses I could find. I confess, I expected to find only two Orcs, but there are four."

"There should be only three, but the big fool refused to leave me behind," said the old man.

Freida turned to the old Orc. "You're a lot stronger than I was when they came for me. There's still breath in you, you can be useful." She turned to face Rakka. "You have weapons?"

"I do, Lady, but daggers only."

"Can you use a sword?"

"I can."

"Rakka, you've chosen a mate who is always getting into trouble. Sadly, he's also one of my greatest friends. I have few friends, and I cherish those I do have. He needs a lot of protecting so you'll be a busy woman." She pulled a sword from her pack.

"I made this short sword for myself as a second blade, but I find I have no real need of it. I prefer both hands on the hilt of my long sword. This is made of the same metal as the other, it's my bonding gift to you. Use it well to defend his back when I'm not there to do it."

"By all the powers, Rakka," rumbled Drakkat. "The Lady offers you a mighty gift. It's mate, the sword that cannot know defeat, rides at her own shoulder. She's made only two such blades."

Stunned, Rakka accepted the short sword. The instant she touched it she felt it come to life in her hand, the blade glowing, almost dancing with delight, an itch for battle. "Lady, I ..."

"Swing it about, get the feel of it," said Freida.

Rakka made a few test swings and grinned with delight. The sword seemed to become weightless when in motion. With ease she lopped off a thick hardened branch from the dead tree. "By all the gods. Lady, this is a mighty gift. I swear I'll use it to defend Drakkat and his people for as long as I draw breath."

Sinking to one knee before Freida, she bowed her head. Freida took her arm and raised her up. "Kneel to my sister only, Rakka. As a slave I spent far too much time on my knees, I will ask that of no other. Stand and face me as a friend."

"Freida, why?" asked Drakkat.

"You've a good friend, Drakkat, but you're always getting into trouble. Besides, you did say you wanted a bride who could defeat your brother's mate." She sighed and let her shoulders slump. "I sense trouble brewing in the snows, my friend. Perhaps it's nothing, but better to be ready. When the mage said you were on your way home with a bride, I knew who the blade was for."

She turned to Rakka. "It's an odd thing, Rakka. When I made the first one it was a part of me from the instant I touched it, but not so that one. That one lay quiet at my side, waiting for another hand. I saw it come to life for you, as my own does for me. The blade was meant for you, you and no other.

"Come. The day grows old while we blather away about nothing. You, up onto the horse with the child. We'll stay on the ground in case of trouble." The old Orc was startled at her strength as she took his arm to help boost him onto the horse. Drakkat tossed the child up and settled her with her grandsire.

Freida patted the horse's muzzle then led the way, Drakkat and Rakka brought up the rear. Two days later the monsters attacked.

Once again Freida was leading the way with Drakkat and Rakka behind. A dozen or more wolflike creatures suddenly leaped from the trees to be met with Freida's war cry as she cast aside her cloak.

The beast weren't even close to the horses when she met them, sword in hand. She screamed her challenge again as she slew them. They were fast and strong, and insanely savage, but they couldn't touch her, nor could they get past her. The sword flashed and sang as it sliced easily through flesh and bone as she slew them.

The ones that attacked from the other side fared no better as they faced Drakkat's battle axe and Rakka's new sword. Together they waded into the enemy and the monsters fell before them. But more came, trying to get past them to the horses and the weaker members of the party.

In the thick of it Rakka found herself fighting beside a half naked Elf. Freida had dispatched those who'd come at her, tossed aside her tunic, and joined the others as they fought the larger party. With the addition of the third warrior the monsters broke and fled. As they did one pitched forward, an arrow in his back. Freida looked back to see the old Orc, still atop the horse, holding a bow. She grinned as she gave him a raised fist salute.

It was over. The child had reached the ground and found Freida's tunic. Shyly she brought it to the heavily muscled Elf woman who smiled and pulled it back on. "I see now why you throw aside your clothes and don't wear armor," said Rakka. "The blade moves too fast, and the clothing constricts you."

"Indeed so. Drakkat, Rakka is a truly fierce warrior. You've chosen well, my friend. Come, family, let's be away from this place so the ravens can enjoy their feast." With that she swept her cloak about her shoulders once again and led off as though nothing unusual had happened. The next day they sighted the Orc village in the fields before Fugitive.

Freida laid her hand on Drakkat's huge shoulder. "I'll leave the horses for you to deal with. I have to get back to the forge, I'm damn near frozen to death."

Rakka just shook her head as she watched Freida walk away toward the walls of the small town. "Drakkat, what's her story? I thought I'd seen fierce warriors before, but nothing like her. Even as we fought side by side she terrified me."

"She was a slave, a childhood friend of Queen Ariel. The friendship was discovered, Freida was beaten badly and often, then sold to an especially cruel man. Her's was a life of torment and pain until L'ark found her and brought her out.

"She was nearly dead then, but the Dwarves took her in and kept her safe and warm by the forge. She became a smith, and one night the dreams came to her, taught her how to make the god blades. Freida won't leave the forge, not even to follow and fight beside Ariel. Coming for us was as far from that forge as she's been since her rescue.

"Princess Frieda brought you a mighty gift, girl, and she'll make you a fierce ally. That's also why she came to us and gave you the blade. You're the chieftain's mate now, and nobody in their right mind will defy you, not with that blade at your side, or the Lady Blacksmith as a friend."

"So, she's taken pains to help me take and hold my place. That woman's a friend of yours, my man, she's done this for you."

"She has, but she's also offered you the hand of friendship. She rarely does that."

"I suspected as much. Drakkat, I'll do all in my power to be a worthy friend to her, and to be a support to you. The Elf Queen and the Warrior who can't be defeated, as well as Mearith the Merciless. My chieftain, you have some mighty allies."

"And now I have a mate who's their equal. Come, girl, let's go home and get a fire up in the house. I'm freezing."

Back to Argar

It took two days of slogging through deep snows, but Kern and his party reached the hidden wagon. They camped for the night and Kern awakened to see the Elf Queen and Mearith sitting by the fire preparing meat. Dera shrieked as he tossed aside the cloak they'd slept under and struggled to his feet. "My Queen."

Ariel laughed as Dera pulled the cloak tight to herself. "Dera, it's a poor mate who'd toss you into the freezing snows first thing in the morning." With sudden wide eyes Dera started to rise. "No, no, girl, stay there, stay warm. Kern, come up to the fire and tell us of your adventures."

"My queen, how did you find us? What brings you here?"

"We checked in at the gates of Shotar," replied Ariel. "Lora told us of your need to get the horses to a better place and where you planned to go."

Kern carefully lowered himself to the ground by the fire. "So, all is well at the gates?"

"All is well, Kern," replied Mearith. "Lora fought at my side at the gates of Elanda long ago. She'll see the task done, my young friend, worry not. The concern I have is all the horses. Is there any hope at all of them surviving the winter?"

"These are Northwood ponies, Lady Mearith. Survive the cold winters is what they do. My fear is deep snows that hinder them. I hope to find the wind has swept the fields of Argar free of most of it so they can forage."

"And the wagon?"

"It's loaded with food and tools, Lady, that, and people from the gates of Shotar. I hope to get them to Argar. There is yet another wagon to be found. It's filled to the brim with food we hope to deliver there as well. The problem is the big horses. The snow is deep, and they struggle to pull the wagon through the drifts."

"You've set yourself a hard task, Kern," said Ariel. "Long will be your journey at this pace."

"I know, my queen, but there's no battle to reach, only safety for these few people."

"I'm curious, why have you brought so many infirm and weak? Could you not find stronger folk to help you?"

Kern sighed and poked at the fire for a moment. "Lady, there is little food, if any coming from within the city of Shotar. As it is, the strongest of the refugees have pushed the weaker away from the gates, preventing them from reaching any food or shelter at all. Lady, we brought this upon these people. Should I have left them to die in the snows? Do I abandon them now to their fate?"

"No, Kern, you did right. We'll help you reach Argar, for that's now our destination as well. What think you, Mearith, my heart? Can we help these folk?"

Mearith's eyes twinkled with merriment. "I'm sure we can, my delight. We can break trail through the drifts so the horses have less work to do."

"Us? Break the trail? On foot?"

Mearith was all innocence and wide eyes as she grinned at Ariel. "I can think of no other way, can you?"

Ariel laughed as she lightly poked Mearith in the ribs. "Yes I can, and so can you. Kern, I see you have several draft horses in the herd. My joking companion and I will lead them through the drifts first, you follow with the shorter ponies, then the wagon follows on the beaten trail."

Kern nodded. "I hadn't thought of using the big horses to break the trail. I was holding them back to help with the wagon if needed."

"There's not a farmer among you, is there?" grunted the old Orc as he joined them by the fire. Ariel arched an eyebrow at him so he went on. "Did you savages leave a single barn or shed standing?"

"Why?" asked Kern.

"Because, my young friend, there should be snow runners for the wagons there."

"Snow runners?"

"Long slats. We take the wheels off the wagon and install the runners. The wagon then slides across the snows far more easily."

"You're joking."

"I'm not. How the blazes do you people think farm folk move about in winter?"

Kern chuckled and shook his head. "In truth, I hadn't put any thought into that at all." He clapped the old Orc on the shoulder. "See? I told you there'd be uses for you yet. So, you know what to look for. We'll take a few warriors with us and go foraging for wagon runners. The rest can camp here for now."

"You may not have to go far, Kern," said Mearith. "There's a burned out farm just over that hill, we saw it as we arrived at your camp. There appears to be a fallen barn partially intact and a shed still standing. I'll go with this fine fellow to show the way. You stay here with the horses."

"We'll both go," said Ariel. "We'll borrow a couple of those big horses to help bring back the runners if we can find them."

Off they went, two big draft horses following along. The sun was high overhead by the time they reached the place. The barn and shed were as Mearith had said. While the horses pawed through the snows looking for grass to eat, the Elves and Orc dug away the drifts from the door and entered the shed.

They were in luck, there were two sets of runners stored in the shed. They carried them outside, lashed them together, then hooked them to the horses' harness. It was late in the day when they returned with the horses pulling the makeshift sled, two Elves and an Orc aboard and enjoying the ride. By the time darkness had fallen, the runners were installed on the wagon, and all was ready to move on when dawn returned.

Next day, with the wagon mounted on broad runners it was easier for the horses to pull it along and they made better time. By high sun they'd found an open area where the wind had swept the field clear of snow. Kern called for a halt to let the horses graze. They camped in the open that night then set out again in the morning.

Uneasy, Mearith spoke softly to Ariel, then dropped back as the party moved slowly away on the long march to Argar. It was late in the day when she returned, running swiftly across the snowy fields. She was being pursued by a dozen strange looking creatures. Ariel had seen them before and began shouting orders.

Mearith reached the wagon just as a hail of arrows from Kern and his dozen Elves slew half her pursuers. Ariel's bow slew another and then another. The few who reached the wagon met Mearith's blades and died on them.

"Mearith, are you harmed, are there more?"

"No to both questions, my delight. Ariel, I think that, once we reach Argar, you and Trelanth should take a hard look at what the Geni might be up to. These things have never been so far from the mountains before. I sense an evil hand at work here."

"As do I, my heart. It shall be as you desire. I too would like to know what's afoot here. Kern, get them moving, I'd like to reach Argar as quickly as possible."

It wasn't going to be that easy. Two days later they ran into a war band of professional soldiers. The dozen Elves leaped to their mounts, but the taller horses had the advantage in the deep snow. Their few numbers didn't look to have a chance against sixty mounted soldiers.

Ariel was shocked at what happened next as the warriors on their heavy horses began their charge. A wild scream of challenge burst from Kern's lips as he urged his horse forward. As one the wild Narthwood ponies leaped ahead to follow. The Elves clinging to the backs of their mounts followed Kern's example as he slid over the pony's side, hanging on with his good leg and an arm around the horse's neck.

Nearing the charging war horses Kern turned aside as best he could. The Elves loosed their arrows, but to little effect. The riders all wore heavy armor. The smaller horses were soon floundering in the snow and the big horses gaining as they followed the broken trail. Only then did Ariel notice how Kern's people had spread out the attackers.

At least half the attackers came on, straight for the wagon. Ariel leaped to the seat, bow in hand. The warrior's armor was no shield against the magic of her bow. One by one they fell to the Elf Queen.

While Ariel plied her bow, Mearith charged right at the soldiers. Ducking beneath the blows she stabbed at the horses causing them to rear and plunge into their comrades. A moment later a man was down and she filled his empty saddle.

No man nor Orc was Mearith's equal in a fight from horseback. Between her and Ariel's bow they managed to set the men into chaos. Mearith was swarmed, and abandoned the horse to create havoc from below, and then she was in another saddle, on the attack once again.

One rider broke past Mearith to charge at the wagon. Just before he reached it his horse slammed into an invisible wall, throwing the rider to the ground. Ariel was down off the wagon and up on the war horse's back in an instant. As she took the fallen reins, the beast screamed a challenge, reared up then charged at the men trying to pen Mearith in.

Ariel's mount slammed into the others from the side and her magic blade flashed right and left, slipping past shield and plate armor. The blows sent her way bounced off an unseen shield and no harm befell her.

Less than a dozen warriors faced her now, and they pulled closer together for defense against these fierce Elves. As they closed ranks, Ariel's mount screamed another challenge, reared up, pawing the air, then leaped to the charge. Again she slammed into them, their swords sliding harmlessly away from her magic shield.

Mearith's stolen charger slammed into the melee from the other side. It wasn't magic that kept the blades from her body, it was her speed, strength, and deadly accuracy with her own swords. She cut her way through them until the last three in the group turned to flee. She and Ariel rode them down and slew them.

As the last one fell Ariel turned to find Kern and his people. A smile reached her lips as she began to understand what she was seeing. Kern and Dera stood back to back in the open, but no rider could get near them. Kern, his eyes closed and his arms spread wide, was talking to the horses. No matter what the riders did, their mounts would not approach the lame man on the ground.

Men threw spears and knives at him, but Kern seemed to know and batted them aside. The warriors who pursued the rest of the Elves were also completely frustrated. The Elves had abandoned their ponies and run through the snows. They easily darted aside from the blows sent their way, and the big horses soon tired and slowed down.

Once a running Elf gained enough distance he turned and loosed another arrow. There were barely a dozen riders left when Ariel and Mearith slammed into them from behind. As night fell, so did the last of the unknown attackers.

Mearith and the Elves began the task of dispatching the wounded and looting the bodies. They tried to question one, but they couldn't understand the language. Kern and Dera gathered up the horses, both their wild ponies and the war horses. They took what gold, weapons, and food they could find then left the dead where they fell.

The fire crackled cheerily, but there was little cheer in the camp. "How many did we lose?" asked Ariel.

"We lost a single Bornani, my queen," replied Kern. "However, we took a number of wounds. We need to get our folk to Argar, and quickly. The problem is, we already have a wagon load of people, and the next wagon is full of food. We'll need that before the snows leave the lands."

"I know, my friend. Mearith, my heart, what do you suggest we do?"

"We put as many people as can ride on the new horses. Use the big war horses to break the trail. We should also push hard. That's twice we've been attacked. It's starting to annoy me."

"And me as well," sighed Ariel. "The thing I'd like most to know is, where did these men come from? What's happened that so many men at arms are loose, how did they get past Tanis? Is Argar still there?"

"Perhaps you should take a look, my love."

Ariel nodded then squirmed a bit to get more comfortable before closing her eyes. No one spoke or moved until she opened her eyes again. "Argar is still there, unharmed, and unaware of what happened. Somehow these men passed the town by, and no Elf or mage knew of their passing.

"So, the question remains, where did these men come from? Why are the wolflike creatures down from the mountains? I need to get to Argar. I need Trelanth to guard me while I investigate these things and see what the Geni are up to.

"When the sun breaks the spell of darkness we set out for Argar and we push hard." The others nodded their agreement then sought their blankets.

As they settled down for the night Ariel noticed one old man gazing thoughtfully at the cloak he'd been given, turning the pin in his hands with a strange fondness. She arose and went to him. "What troubles you about that cloak pin, my friend?"

Startled, the man tried to rise to a kneeling position, but she caught his arm to stop him. She settled down beside him and nodding, he spoke. "Lady, this is a Dorian pin."

"Dorian pin?"

"Lady, when I was just a boy, men came to my village at the seashore. They took slaves and I was forced to spend a few years as a cabin boy. One night we were swamped in a terrible storm. Only I survived to reach land. That was the island of Doria.

"I spent many happy years there, learning the ways of farming and fishing. Eventually I chose a mate, but her people objected and so we stole a small boat and fled back to this land. We moved inland, far from the coast and any chance of reprisals.

"Lady, the men you fought this day are king's men from Doria. See, here on the pin is the king's sign. They must have come through the portal."

"Portal?"

"On Doria there was an old Geni mage who often appeared with strange things he'd taken from distant lands. It was said he possessed a portal that would take him wherever he wanted to go and bring him back again. The tale goes that his ancestor captured the portal from the palace of the Elf Queen when she broke the world."

Mearith and a few others had overheard much of his tale. "If this is true," said Mearith, "why would he send men at arms out here into the middle of nowhere?"

"I have no idea," mused Ariel, "but, that would explain how they managed to get past Trelanth without her knowledge."

Mearith nodded. "Perhaps tomorrow I'll follow their trail back to see where they landed, and to make sure there are no more coming."

"I wonder, could they have arrived here, but this wasn't the intended landing site," mused Ariel.

"Ariel?"

"My heart, I highly doubt any Geni would be able to fully control one of Queen Onlay's magical objects. I also wonder why they were sent at all. If it was an attempt to aid the Geni, would not many more be sent?"

"There would be no more to send," said the old fellow. "Dorians are mostly farmers, and fishers. The king employs a hundred men at arms to keep the peace, but that's all. With these gone all he'll have left are his personal guards."

Mearith thought for a moment. "My friend, this king, is he a Geni perhaps?"

"Yes, he's a Geni, or so they say. I never laid eyes on him or the mage myself."

Ariel sighed deeply. "Ah well, it's a puzzle for another day. Right now I need sleep. Thank you, my friend, you've been more help than you know."

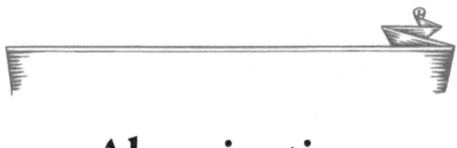

Abomination

While the queen fought against heavy odds, Eline and Ethor sat by an open fire, smiling with delight, their upper bodies moving to the beat of the drums and the wild dancing of a dozen Elves. It was an old tradition of the Elves, its origins lost deep in the mists of time. The idea was to send out the energy of joy and warmth to entice the spirits of spring to return.

While war raged in the open lands far below, the Elves who were the garrison of the way station had spent the long summer and autumn preparing for winter. They'd also taken out the time to make a few drums, flutes, and bowlala, a large bow played by striking the string with a stick, the string being tightened or loosened by the bending of the bow.

As the dancers tired others leaped to their feet and joined in. It went on through much of the night, the feasting as well. It was a welcome change for the Borni warriors who'd fought in the wars below, and a joyful amazement for the newly freed Bornani.

Eline smiled wistfully as she watched them join in. This night they would dance and feast. On the morrow they'd begin a winter of training as Elvish warriors. If they were going to be spending the winter in this high mountain valley, they'd spend it in training. Besides, that would keep her mind off a young Elf still in the wide lands far below.

"Thoughts on Tanis?" asked Ethor.

"Dammit, Ethor. Am I that easy to read?"

"I'm a mage, I know things."

"Shut up, Ethor. All right. I've waited and waited for the pull to claim me, especially since we returned to Elandor, but ...."

"The ways of the Pull are mysterious, even to a mage," he replied. "Do you plan to speak to him?"

"No. I know him, Ethor. I'm certain he feels as I do, but holds back in fear that, should he speak, the Pull could one day snatch me away. Sadly, I do agree with the reasoning, for should I bond with him, then lose him to the Pull ..."

"It truly grieves me to find so much hesitation and fear among the queen's war leaders. I ..." he ducked away from the swipe she took at him, and further threats from her were forestalled as a young female Bornani grabbed him and pulled him into the dance.

As dawn returned light to the world, the drums fell silent and everyone went to their rest. Again Eline sought out Ethor. "Something's moving out there, my friend, and I get the feeling we're not going to like it. I've sent scouts out, but ..."

"I'll take a look. Put everybody on alert just in case." She nodded and trotted away.

Three days passed with the tension growing in the camp. Ethor rarely stopped his search, but came up empty. Finally he approached her. "You're right, Eline, something's out there, but I can't find it. I feel the push of the Geni mages, hiding whatever it is, but I don't know how or why, or what it is we face."

"Then it's time we changed tactics. Your specialty is masking spells. Hide us, Ethor. Keep us hidden from prying eyes, both the way station as well as the Elves in the forest. If we can't find them, then they should have to work at finding us.

"Make us vanish into the snows and the Borni will spy them out, whatever they are. We'll find them, lay traps, misdirect them, and make sure they never see the flowers of Spring."

"Eline, be careful. I get a sense of a madness unchained. Whatever's out there, the Geni have set it loose, and they mask its movements, but they have no control of it." She nodded and trotted away.

Days later a scout caught sight of something that shouldn't exist. It looked like a tall Orc crossed with some kind of reptile. It carried weapons and wore leather armor. There were a dozen or more, and they marched in single file to hide their numbers, constantly stopped to sniff the air, then moving on.

Carefully the scout pulled back then fled silently through the forest. No matter what, there is no creature alive more silent or swift in the forest than a Borni warrior. He raced on, stopped to warn the next scout then sped on. A few more stops and warnings later he reached Eline and Ethor. "They look like Ogres crossed with some form of reptile," he said as he finished his report.

"Ogres blended with minor demons," replied Ethor. "Now I know why I couldn't see them before. I didn't know what to look for."

"There's more, Sir," said the Borni scout as he regained his breath. "They're wearing amulets of invisibility like the pig men wore before. My own turned red, that's how I knew something was about in the forest."

"Where are they?" asked Eline.

"Approaching the first bend in the river."

She nodded. "Ethor, take a closer look now, is there any other danger lurking about?"

"No. I can see all except for that area by the river's bend."

"Then we go. Hide our passage, old friend. We'll give them a welcome they didn't expect. We go!"

She trotted away with the scout right beside her. A wave of Elves silently followed closely. As they neared the place they split apart, a full fifty Elves to the left side and yet another to the path on the right.

A short while later the invaders marched silently into the trap. The leader stopped and held up a hand to halt the column. His massive head swung around and around, testing the air, his eyes searching. A grunted word and weapons slipped into every hand as they moved back to back in a defensive position.

They waited, but nothing happened. No bird sang, no squirrel chattered in a tree. The forest held its breath as they waited. Eventually his patience ran out. He couldn't detect anything, hear anything, so, slowly he stepped out, back onto the trail. As soon as the column stretched out again, a hail of arrows felled all but three of his men.

The leaders keen senses heard a soft sound, the sound of an arrow being drawn against the bow. He shouted the warning and dove to the ground even as the arrows flew. Only he and three others rose from the ground with shields raised.

He howled in rage and frustration as the next volley of arrows came in low, piercing their legs and laming every man. They began to fall, the shields breaking formation as the leg injuries took their toll. As a shield lowered and gave an opening, an arrow filled the gap. Soon they all lay on the snow, the leader the only one still drawing ragged breaths.

A female Elf approached and squatted just out of his reach. "We have fought before, Ogre. Far in the past did we fight. It grieves me, what the Geni have done to you, what they forced you to become."

The creature hissed and tried to lunge at her with his sword. The blow was clumsy and weak, she easily batted it aside. "Tell me, are there more of you?"

It drew several ragged breaths. "I know not, Elf. At the end, when the witch slew us all, the masters put some to sleep for a future time. That time is now."

With that its life slipped away and it relaxed into the blood-stained snow. Eline rose to her feet. "Ethor, did you hear that?"

"I did. I have a speaking stone in my pack. I'll contact Trelanth and she can inform the queen. I'll redouble my efforts to keep this way station hidden."

She nodded her agreement. "Loot the bodies for anything useful then leave them for the wolves and ravens."

It took many days, but the Elves combed the valley from one end to the other. They found no more enemies and so they returned to the way station and their training.

AS THE LAST MUTATED Ogre fell in the mountain forest, a richly dressed Geni howled in rage. He hurled a platter across the room then ordered a slave to clean up the mess and bring him more food. "Another failure, mage. What do you have to say for yourself?" snarled Kratac, King of the Geni, ruler of all the land.

"I say watch your foolish tongue, you inbred imbecile," snarled the old Geni who rose from the seeing glass and began pacing about the room. "Yes, the demon hybrids failed. I suspected they would as soon as I realized a mage was with them. This man is strong, and I can't pierce his shield. Only once the battle was joined was I able to see.

"So, we awakened them and they failed, as did the wolf-orc hybrids. However, we're starting to get somewhere."

"Oh really," sulked the king as he began to devour the new platter of food the slave had brought. "The Elves are at the gates, not a single hunter has returned from the forest, the army we sent to Fugitive didn't return, and yet another defeat this day. Pray tell me, how does the mightiest mage in my kingdom see this as progress?"

The mage shot him a look, but sighed and let his shoulders slump. "Yes, they're at the gates and in the forest, but not the great armies she's shown us. I think she's trying to fill all the cities in the land with refugees, and thus is spread too thin to make any concerted attack. We're quite safe within these walls."

"So, why would she do this? What does she hope to gain?" asked the king.

"She's filling the cities with refugees, trying to use up our resources, starve us out."

"Surely we have enough to last the winter." There was a sudden look of deep concern on the king's face.

"Not if you keep eating enough for a dozen or more. At this rate the storehouses will be empty long before the snows melt in spring."

"Then we must put the people on rations."

"We've already done that, and thrown every Dwarf, Human, or Orc that can't fight, out the gates so we don't have to feed them. However, I doubt it will be enough."

The king was deeply concerned. "What are we going to do?"

The mage sneered as he turned from the seeing glass to face the king. "What would his mighty majesty like us to do?"

The king shivered and moved away from the table laden with food to stand closer to the fire. "Everything possible, everything you can. We must get control of this situation. We need to get those slaves back, and we need to regain control of these lands. By all the gods, she's made alliances and is building cities of her own, and yet, you do nothing. Release a few failed experiments from the ancestors? Surely there is more than that you could do."

A look of pure malice reached the mage's face as he advanced on the king. "Are you giving me full command?"

The king turned away to the fire, trying to retain a shred of dignity and the illusion of his royal status. "Yes, I give you full command. I don't care what you have to do; but get this under control while there are a few Geni left alive. You know she wants to kill us all, so do something about her."

The mage's smile was cold and cruel as he bowed slightly to the king. "As you command, Sire. Enjoy your meal." With that he withdrew from the room, calling for his mages and assistants.

"Sir?" asked a young mage.

"You heard me, unleash them all. Every single failed experiment and abomination we have access to, release them all. Expel all the families of the remaining fighters, we've haven't enough food to keep them through the winter."

"Sir, if we do that the men at arms will revolt."

"Not if you make an extreme example of the first one to open his mouth. We are the Geni, we rule here. This is our land by right of capture. We keep only those who are of use to us, the rest fend for themselves. Now get busy.

"Arca!"

The tall Geni in the mage's robe bowed slightly as he turned to the royal mage. "Sir?"

"Contact the other cities, tell them what we're doing here, tell them to do the same. We must survive until the spring with strong armies." The man bowed slightly again then turned and left the room.

The Royal mage then approached his assistant who was bent over a seeing crystal. "Well, how did our adventure with the Dorians go?"

The woman swallowed hard before answering. "Badly."

"What's that? Speak up."

"I said it went badly, Sir."

"Explain."

"The Dorian mage was an incompetent fool. He didn't have the power to complete the task and refused our help. He managed to snatch away nearly a hundred fighting men, but didn't have the strength to get them to Shotar. He collapsed and died from the strain, dropping the men in the snows about three or four days ride away."

"So, they'll get here eventually. They're strong and well trained troops. We need each and every one of them."

"Sir, those men are all dead."

"What? What happened?"

"For some reason, she was there."

"She? The Elf Queen? She killed them all?"

"Yes, Sir. Somehow she must have known and was waiting for them. Perhaps it was she who killed the ancient mage of Doria, dropping those men right in her path."

"Yes, I believe you're right about that. This one truly is the Witch of Elanda returned."

"Sir, what are we going to do?"

"An oath of silence, now. None can know this." The woman swallowed again as she nodded. "You must prepare in secret. I will soon bring you a map to a tower, it's on my ancestor's home in the waste lands. When the snows melt and the Elves come, you and I will translocate ourselves there.

"There we can survive and prepare. The Witch cannot be defeated, there's no hope of that. She will drive the last of our people to those lands where we will be waiting. Better to rule in the wasted lands than to die here in a battle that is already lost. Do you understand what you must do?"

"Yes, Master, I understand. As soon as I have the location I'll begin slowly teleporting as much of our supplies as I can without arousing suspicion. Sir, will we not take any of the others with us?"

"No. We dare not. We must leave them here to confront the witch and keep her attention diverted while we make good our escape." Again she nodded, then began to make a mental list of the things she would need to take with them.

A Glimmer of Understanding

Tanis was in his usual place at his war table, enjoying a bowl of stew when Trelanth came striding into the inn. "Trelanth, what is it?"

"The queen comes. They're days away, but they've just fought a hard battle."

"A battle? Where?"

"On the road to Shotar. My Lord Tanis, somehow a large number of mounted warriors, over a half a hundred strong, appeared and attacked them."

"Half a hundred warriors? Where did they come from? How did they get onto the road to Shotar without us knowing about it? How is it the queen is on that road?"

"Forgive me, my Lord, for I have failed you. Those men got past us, and I knew it not. The queen was at the walls of Shotar during the storm, and has journeyed this way with Kern and a few others. Lora remains at the gates with the Reavers. It's my guess the snows there are too deep for Kern's horses to be effective, and so he returns to us."

"Hmm. Yes, that makes sense. You say the queen and her small band have defeated the warriors, so we're all right there. Can you find out how they got past us? Are there more of them wandering about without our knowledge?"

"I don't believe so. I've looked with every sense I have and all the power available to me, and I found none."

Tanis nodded slowly. "All right, so, Queen Ariel is a few days away yet. She'll have wounded with her, most likely. Grace."

"Yes, Lord Tanis?"

"Any chance we could borrow a couple of those sliding wagons you people use? I'd like to go out to meet the queen and help her on the way. At least we can beat down a trail for her horses to follow."

Grinning, the woman rose to her feet and headed for the door. "I'll get a couple ready for you."

He thanked her then turned to Trelanth to see her focused on a talking stone. Only she could hear the voice so he waited until she was finished. She suddenly looked up and met his eyes. "I'll be going with you to meet the queen."

With a nod Tanis swept up his cloak and sword. As he reached the door the serving woman stepped in his path and handed him a small sack. "Food for the road, My Lord Tanis."

"You're a precious jewel," he grinned as he kissed her cheek. "Were you not already bonded I'd run off with you myself."

"Get on with you, you young fool." She blushed, but he was already out the door.

"What is it, Trelanth?" he asked as she climbed to the wagon seat beside him.

"Eline has faced an enemy from the past this day. Ogres crossed with minor demons."

"Eline..."

Trelanth patted his arm. "She's fine, my Lord. They defeated the enemy. As the last one died it told her that, as the War of World Breaking ended, the Geni put what warriors and creations they had, to sleep, awaiting a future time of need. They're awakening them now. The queen must be warned."

In answer he lightly flicked the reins, urging the big horses to greater speed.

WHILE TANIS RODE OUT to meet the queen, Lora was watching something else from the edge of the forest. The great gates of Shotar opened and the refugees surged toward them. Instead of a supply of food they faced armed men who drove them back. Intrigued by the shouts of rage and protest, Lora and two others slipped closer, moving along the wall just out of sight.

When they reached a point where they could see, they stopped in shock. The armed men were fighting the refugees, but some had turned to defend the weak. Slowly, but surely a large number of people were forced out of the gates with one lone man at arms still trying to defend them. He was being forced back by several of his former comrades.

Suddenly arrows flew and three men fell wounded. The cry went up. "Elves! The Elves are attacking. Close the gates. Close the gates." More arrows followed the men at arms back through the gate as they dragged their wounded comrades inside.

The gates were shut and braced. The men atop the walls looked below, but no Elves could be seen. They dared not throw down the stones and oil unless they had a target. The supplies were limited and being saved to be used against a full scale attack.

Down below the lone warrior stood protectively before a woman and three children. He saw the three Elves salute him then slip away. Sweeping the youngest of the children up into his arms, he set out slowly to follow the Elves.

As he reached the trees the three Elves stepped out with drawn bows. Gently he set the child down and dropped his shield to the snows. "Kill me if you must, Elf, but spare my family, I beg you. They're innocent in all this."

They gazed at each other for a moment then the Elf woman stepped forward, swept the small child into her arms and turned away. "Come." Her two companions each picked up a child and led the way.

It was a long hike, but they eventually reached a camp of close to a hundred Elves. The leader set the child down near the fire then passed her some food.

The warrior was surprised to see an Elf he hadn't noticed before, drop his shield beside him. The leader spoke to the others in a language he couldn't understand then they vanished into the trees, heading for the gates of Shotar.

She then turned to him and his family. "Sit, eat, warm yourselves. I will return soon, then we'll talk." With that she vanished into the forest.

Another Elf approached. "Eat, there's plenty of food. When you're warm and well fed, there's a shelter beneath that tree. You can sleep there if you wish."

"Why are you people helping us?"

The Elf laughed. "I have no idea at all, but Lora will have her reasons. We'll ask her when she returns."

"Where did she go?" asked the eldest child.

"She went to take food to those at the gates. She'll be back soon. Rest now and eat." He patted the child's shoulder then went to another task.

The day was well along when the leader returned. She came to them at the fire and sat beside the warrior. "Now, my friend, tell me your name and of what has happened inside the walls."

"I'm Garret," he replied. "They came to us at the barracks, three mages. They ordered us to drive all the families of the men at arms out through the gates. The Geni refuse to feed anyone who can't wield a sword.

"Several of us objected, but the mages killed the two nearest them. Those men died a terrible death. They told us we'd all meet the same fate if we didn't obey our masters. I shut my mouth and followed orders.

"As we herded the helpless toward the gates, I moved closer to my own family. When the gates opened I turned to defend them as did a few others. The gates aren't wide enough for a full scale battle so we were able to get them out, but, as you saw, I'm the only one to survive, and I won't last long."

"Why do you say that?"

"The Geni mages mark every man at arms. That way they can reach out to punish those they deem unworthy or unwilling."

"Mark, how?"

The man pulled aside his tunic to show a dark mark on his upper chest, just above his heart. The Elf nodded for a moment then took a small amulet from around her neck. "This could hurt." She pressed the amulet against the mark and he hissed in pain. The mark writhed like an animal in torment, but slowly it vanished, leaving a burn scar behind.

The Elf woman returned the amulet to its place about her neck then sighed. "So they ejected all the families of the fighting men?" The man just nodded. "How strong are your loyalties to them?"

"Loyalty? To those who would have me sell my life for them, yet would make me force my own family out into the snows to freeze or starve? None, I say. Not one lick. My loyalty now is to this woman and the children she bore me, to her and no other."

To his great surprise Lora grinned and turned to his wife. "Well then, good woman, my name is Lora. It seems you have a loyal man at arms. You and your children have need of food and shelter for the winter. I have need of good fighters. I propose an alliance. I'll provide the food and shelter in exchange for the services of your man at arms in my fight with the Geni."

Wide eyed the woman looked to her husband then back to the Elf. "You're serious?"

The merriment was easy to read in Lora's eyes. "Oh yes, quite serious."

Another glance at her husband saw him nodding his agreement. The woman smiled in return. "Agreed then, good Elf. My name is Ellen.

Lady, we can't thank you enough for what you've done for us. We'll do everything we can to help you."

"Wonderful. For now, Garret, your task will be to protect this woman and her children. When you've had a few days to rest we'll take another look at this. In the long run I want to get you to the town of Argar. They have need of strong folk and will welcome you."

The man nodded. "Lady, why did you help us?"

She gave him her full attention as she replied. "We're not the enemy here, my friend, nor are you. The Geni are the enemy. We drove as many as we could into the city to use up their resources, as they did to us so many ages ago. Now that they've shown their true nature, we want to help you rebuild your lives.

"The idea here is simple. Argar needs farmers, skilled tradesmen, smiths, and more. Elves, humans, Orcs, Dwarves, and more will all live and work in harmony. No slaves, ever again. You say your loyalty is to this woman? She and her children will be welcomed in Argar, so I'm sure she'll agree to the terms of life there."

"Of course I will."

"Then that's the plan for you. When the snows leave the lands we'll get you there. You'll have a home and we'll have new allies."

"Lady," said Ellen, "there are many more families cast out this day. You could gain a lot more allies by taking in those families."

Lora turned and smiled at her. "And I wish that I could do just that. We'll do what we can to provide them with food. However, that isn't my assigned purpose here."

"May I ask what that purpose might be?" asked Garret.

"No hunter from the city will return, but his cloak and boots will warm a refugee at the gates. If armed men are sent out to forage, I make that as unpleasant for them as I can. Any man at arms who enters the forest will not return."

"Since my patron has made an alliance with you, am I to be set this task as well?" asked Garret.

"Can you do it? Will you fight, kill, your former comrades at arms?"

"To keep my family alive and safe? Yes."

She nodded then gripped his shoulder. "I won't ask that of you unless I have no choice. For now you'll be assigned to the camp to gather firewood and to defend it as necessary. Get some rest. Tomorrow will be a new day." She patted his shoulder, winked at the woman, then rose and walked away.

BACK AT THE GATE, LORA was watching the madness. The refugees who had managed to create some form of shelter were defending those shelters from those who were newly ejected from the gates. Some few fought, but most just cowered away, getting pushed further and further from the gates and any possible food that might come from within.

She shook her head sadly, for she knew full well, there would be no more food issue from those dark gates. Not now. The ejection of the families told her clearly that already the supplies within were starting to run low.

Worse yet, Lora knew there was little she could do to help them. They'd stayed in the area too long already, the game was growing scarce and it was taking longer and longer to find firewood. She turned to the Elf beside her. "Bralin, What's your assessment?"

"Sadly, Lora, I think it's time to move on. The question is, how many of them can we take with us and how many do we leave here?"

"I'm open to suggestions."

"I hesitate to say it, old friend, but, Kern himself made you leader of a hundred. The decision falls to you."

Lora grinned and lightly punched his arm. "I know. Go back, prepare to move the camp. We'll leave a few scouts here, but we'll retreat a few leagues back towards Argar." He nodded then trotted away.

The next morning they moved out, leaving little or no trace of a camp behind. When they set up a new camp three days closer to Argar the human warrior sought out Lora. "Lady, may I speak?"

"Come, Garret, rest by the fire. Are your people well?"

"They are. No, it's of those left behind I would speak."

"You want to know why we abandoned them. We'd already depleted the game near Shotar, that and we'd been in one place too long. We can do little more for the refugees at those cold gates. Now we must see to our own people.

"Near here is a wagon loaded with edible roots we took from abandoned farms. There is also game aplenty. We'll camp here for the rest of the winter. Scouts are still at the gates of Shotar and a runner is already well on the way to Argar to inform Lord Tanis of our plans. If he has a different task for us, he can send for us here.

"I know you'd like to help those families left behind, but we need to see to our own folk first."

"Understood, Lady, and thank you." He grinned as he rose to his feet. "I'll relay that to my patron."

"She's concerned for her friends?"

"She is that."

Lora gave a deep sigh then nodded. "I'll see if I can devise a way to help more, but I make no promises."

He nodded and returned to his wife at their fire. Lora called a few of the others to her. They spoke for a while then they split up and went to different groups of the other Elves. At length they returned to her and she approached the human family. "Ellen, we must confer."

"Lora?"

"You're concerned about the other families back at the gates. I understand that. Tell me, Garret, is there any chance at all that the Geni will provide some food or shelter for those forced out?"

"None." He sighed and let his shoulders slump. "Not one single chance, not a single scrap of food will they share. That was made plain to us."

"Now comes the big question for both of you. Do you believe that the people behind at the gates would be willing to live in peace with the Elves, to accept us as a free and equal people, to trade with and deal fairly us?"

"What? Well, yes, I ..."

"Carefully, Ellen. Think before you speak. I'm quite certain there are a number of women in that group who've raised a whip to an Elf's back. There are a good number of those former slaves in this company. A few may even recognize former masters. Consider before you speak."

The woman sighed and reached for Lora's hands, gazing earnestly into her eyes. "Lora, you're right about that. I'm sure that man over there remembers me and the harsh words I've spoken to him in the past. I can't undo what was done, nor can the others.

"However, you people have taken us in, fed and nurtured us, treated us as equals, and we have tried to show our gratitude. I, and the others, have had a harsh education in the past year. You've offered me and my family a chance to start over. Can you not do the same for the others?"

"Garret?"

"Lady, if you're willing to make the offer I'll personally gut the first one to betray your trust. Ellen speaks the truth; the past year has provided much education."

Lora nodded and thought for a moment. "All right, here's what we can do, and it's all we can do. My warriors have already agreed to this. In fact, your former slave suggested it.

"The plan is thus. A few remain here to guard the camp while the rest of us return to the gates of Shotar. You, Garret, go among the families there, speak to the people, make certain they understand the new ways, Elves are a free and equal people to be respected.

"Once they understand, tell them we will lead them to a better place. We'll do all we can to provide food and shelter, to help them to a town where they will be welcomed. Their lives in the new town won't be lives of luxury, they will be expected to work beside all the other people. There'll be no slaves to do the work for them.

"Those who are willing to agree, and to be allies of the Elves, bring to us in the forest. We'll guide them here then we'll all move on together. Is this agreeable to you?"

"Oh Lora, will you truly do this? Will you really help those poor families?"

"We will, Ellen, if they're willing. You stay here, but I'll need Garret with me. We leave at dawn."

It took a few days to reach the gates again. Once there, Garret went among the families. They'd been out in the cold for many days without food and were in bad shape. All agreed, as did a number more of people who had been at the gates a lot longer. No more food had come from inside and all were desperate.

Garret led them into the trees, over a hundred weak and struggling people, mostly humans and a few Orcs. Once in the trees the dreaded Elvish raiders appeared and assisted the infirm as best they could. That night the people rested around warm fires and had a small meal.

As the darkness fell the Elf leader rose and spoke. "Hear me, people. My name is Lora. I've brought you here at the request of Garret and his patron, Ellen. They were offered a chance to ally themselves with the Elf Queen, and they chose that road. I now offer the same to you. Ally yourself with the Elves against the Geni and I'll do all in my power to get you to safety, provide food and shelter for you.

"Choose this path and we will leave this place. The road will be long and hard, slowly traveled, but it has hope at the end. There is no hope for you at the gates of Shotar, no hope for succor from the Geni."

"Where are you taking us?" asked a woman who clutched a small child to her.

"To the town of Argar. There is a burned out village near there. We will help you rebuild it if we can. There are fields there to tend, homes can be built, livestock gathered. When the lands warm the queen may call us away to war, but the good people of Argar will surely help you.

"People, I'm truly sorry, but this is all I have to offer you. Yes, it's a slim chance, and a hard life I offer, but it's the best I can do."

"It's a chance at life," replied the woman. "My child will surely die at the gates. My mate didn't defend me as Garret defended Ellen. I must now become the warrior and defend my child's life. The Elves will make far better allies than the Geni. I for one will accept your terms and gladly call you an ally."

There was a round of agreement from the rest of the women and the few older men and Orcs. "So be it," said Lora. "We rest here and eat our fill for a day then we move out. Prepare yourselves as best you can."

Piecing It Together

Even as Lora mulled over the decision to rescue Ellen and family, Tanis reached the queen's party. "Ho, Tanis, well met." called Mearith as she stood in the path of the approaching wagons.

"Lady Mearith, it's good to see you well. Did you lose our queen along the trail, or that her behind me?"

Ariel's sweet laughter floated on the cold winter air as he turned to see her rise from a drift and shake the snow from her cloak. He hopped from the wagon and dropped to one knee before her.

"Rise Tanis, rise and give me the news."

He rose to his feet, smiling. "Lady, much is afoot, and it's Trelanth who brings you news, but I would ask, where is your personal guard?"

"On the march, Tanis. I've sent them ahead to Argar as I had another errand at the gates of Shotar. Did they not arrive?"

"Nay, Lady, they didn't."

"I shall seek for them when we rest for the night, perhaps they've moved on to Magdan. For now we should press on."

"My queen," said Kern as he approached, "perhaps we could camp here for the night. It would give the horses a chance to forage. We can shelter behind the wagons."

"Good idea, Kern. All right then, make camp. Trelanth, come to me and help me get a fire going."

"Yes, my queen."

A fire was soon started and they settled down beside it while the horses found an open spot and began to paw away the snow to reveal the dried grasses below. Trelanth sat with the queen and her companion, Kern and Dera as well.

"Now, Trelanth, tell me what troubles you so."

"Lady, Eline and her people reached the first of the way stations, but could go no further. They will pass the winter there. Recently they fought a small group of creatures long thought gone from these lands. They fought Ogres crossed with minor demons."

"Trelanth?"

"Yes, Lady Mearith, some of them remain. As the last of them lay dying, Eline spoke with it. It told her the Geni had, after the world was broken and the High Born enslaved, put the last of their experimental warriors to sleep, holding them back for future use.

"My queen, the Geni are awakening them all, every abomination they can find, and setting them loose in the lands.

"Moreover, their mages search the world for any means to disrupt things as they now stand. Lady, the men you fought recently were from an island in the western sea, sent to aid Shotar, but the mage who sent them was old, and weak. He fell dead and the warriors appeared where you found them."

"Trelanth, what more do we face?" asked Mearith.

"Ogre hybrids, but not many. Wolf hybrids, all across the lands, some Ogres, swamp giants, but they're dormant until the rains of spring. Some others I cannot name.

"The problem is, I can't locate any of these things until they awaken and begin to move about. As long as they remain asleep they're invisible to us."

"Have you warned the others?"

"I have, my queen. Even as we journeyed to meet you I spoke with my uncle and the rest. All are aware now and on the lookout for anything and everything unusual."

"Then no more can we do at the moment," said the queen. "Forewarned is forearmed. Mearith, you and the Borni have fought all these things before?"

"We have, my delight."

"What are we in for?"

"Trouble, my sweet. All these things are hard to kill, for they all have some magic about them; however, they can be defeated. In our favor, they don't band together and fight as a cohesive unit, a true military force. They're wild, completely savage, uncontrolled, and vulnerable as a result.

"They were brought into being to terrorize and demoralize the enemy. Without a strong Geni they can't be controlled or directed at a particular enemy. This is a desperate attempt to throw us into confusion.

"The Ogres and Ogre Hybrids might work as a unit, but it's hard to say."

"The ones Eline faced did," said Trelanth. "Ladies, there is another problem as well."

"And that is?" asked Ariel.

"My queen, in an attempt to make the supplies last, the Geni are expelling all the poor as well as the families of their warriors from the cities."

"They're what?"

"Yes my queen. I've seen this. There are over a thousand refugees and expelled poor just outside the gates of Magdan now. The same for the rest. The Geni are seizing all the food resources for themselves and their fighting men."

"We've barely reached mid-winter. By all the gods, Mearith, the refugees, all of them plus the families of the men at arms, they'll all die long before spring arrives. What have we done?"

"They've thrown it back in our faces alright," sighed Mearith. "I didn't see that coming. The Geni are more cruel and selfish than I thought."

"And the men at arms more easily cowed than I thought," said Kern. "Did none of them turn on the Geni to defend their families?"

"Many did, but after seeing a few of them burned slowly in a magical fire, dying in torment, most caved in," replied Trelanth. "A few waited then bolted through the gates with their families, but they will be as helpless as the rest in the cold without food or shelter."

"Mearith, what are we to do?"

"What would you like to do, my treasure?"

"Don't do this to me, Mearith, not now. Help me here, I beg you."

Mearith reached for Ariel's hands and held them tightly. "Think like the queen now, my delight. What do you want to do?"

"I want to help them. We brought this upon them, we can't just leave them to starve or die of the cold. Help me here, people. I'm open to any and all suggestions. Tanis, what think you?"

"I agree, my queen. These people have served our purpose, but they can do so no longer as they have been cast out. We know the Geni won't give them food or shelter. Now is the time to make allies of them."

Mearith was grinning at him, and Ariel began to relax. They would devise a plan; she had no doubt. "Tanis, are you suggesting we give these people food and shelter?"

"Yes, Lady Mearith, that is indeed what I'm suggesting."

"And where do you suggest we find these resources?" she asked.

Tanis' grin broadened. "Why, I do believe there should be plenty of shelter and a goodly supply of food within the walls of Magdan. I think we should go there and toss the Geni out into the snows and then bring the refugees inside the walls."

"That was my thought as well," said Mearith.

"So tell me, why did you choose Magdan instead of Shotar or one of the others?" asked Ariel.

"My queen, you badly weakened Magdan when you freed the slaves from within its walls. That city has not fully recovered, it's the weakest of them all. With what we've seen and the numbers of their warriors we've already defeated, there can't be more than two hundred men at arms left in the city. I'm certain a few of them would happily join our ranks to be safely reunited with their families."

"Then so be it," declared Ariel. "We'll take every available warrior and proceed to Magdan. Send a runner ahead to your people, Tanis. Tell them to prepare and to await us near the gates of the city.

"Yes, my friends, we'll turn the tables on these Geni. We'll turn them out into the snows and their minions with them. The refugees will spend the winter safe within the walls, then, when the snows leave the lands, we'll burn Magdan to the ground and help them re-establish the farming villages.

"Trelanth, what do we face for mages in that city of my birth?"

"None of notice, my queen. There were only two of any real power, and one I killed in that last battle with their soldiers. Only his apprentice remains. He will see only what I want him to see until we take the city, then I'll make an end of him."

Ariel smiled brightly. "We have a plan. We'll deliver these good people to Argar then march for Magdan. We begin at first light."

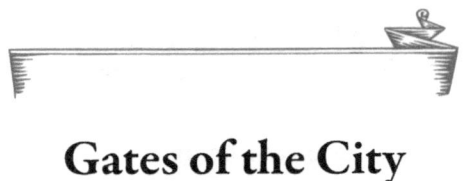

Gates of the City

A t the gates of Shotar the snows were littered with the bodies of the dead. Several of the surviving camps had turned to the dead to use for food. Garret, sighed and averted his eyes as he walked among them.

They all stared at him, for it was obvious he was well fed and healthy as well as heavily armed. First he went among the remaining expelled families, spoke with a few, then continued on as those he spoke to struggled toward the forest along the path he'd made through the snow.

Each woman he spoke to faced the same thing. Their mates had abandoned them and their children. The Elves would help them, but they had to accept the Elves as free people. Faced with starvation and the cold, all were willing enough to agree.

By nightfall over three hundred women and children, as well as elders were gathered in the forest, huddling beside small fires. There was some food distributed among them and they were grateful for that.

Lora stood at the edge of the camp, watching as the women huddled their young close and tried to keep them warm. Bralin approached and stood beside her. "All right, let's hear it."

"Lora, we can't take them to Argar. They've probably got a full house already."

"I know. We'll have to keep them in the forest, move the camp from time to time, but we can keep them alive. By winter's end they'll be strong allies."

"No they won't," said another Elf as he joined them. "They'll spend the winter expecting us to do more, complaining about the lack, and demanding the Elves do more. You're both Borni, you have no experience with these people, we Bornani do. They see Elves as slaves, as lesser beings, born to serve their needs. If we do as you suggest, they'll be convinced that we're doing what we do to help them only as a result of our breeding."

"You're serious?"

"I am, Lora. Even now I can see my old mistress at the fire. I'm surprised she hasn't called out to me to bring her more food and to give her child my cloak."

"So tell me," grinned Bralin, "what'll you do if she does?"

"I'll put a dagger through her evil heart."

Lora's eyes opened wide at that. She reached out to lightly grip his shoulder. "Dead people make poor allies, brother. You have experience I don't have. Help me here, what do you suggest we do?"

The man sighed and shook off the mood. "My first thought is to abandon them here, but that's not our purpose, it won't bring about the desired result. No, there's a better way. Teach them to look after themselves, to survive on their own.

"When I was freed from slavery I was taken into the forest, taught how to survive there. I ate a lot of beetles and roots, but I learned to survive and enjoy the forest. If a woman wants to feed her children she must accompany an Elf to help gather food, hunt for meat, find and gather firewood."

"Teach them to be self-reliant? They spent their lives relying on slaves, now we teach them to rely on themselves?" A sudden grin reached Lora's face. "I like it. Spread the word to the others. We help them, but only if they're willing to help themselves." The man nodded and trotted away.

The next morning it began. The people, mostly women and young children were frightened, but willing. It started with gathering firewood. Wood was gathered from the dead and fallen trees, no fresh was cut. A few scattered cones were shown to be edible. For the next three days they moved slowly through the forest, gathering wood and learning to eat unusual things until they joined with the original small group.

Another snowstorm came then, so they huddled beneath trees, in small numbers. To the amazement of the humans and Orcs, the Elves moved about easily, making sure they all had fire for warmth, and some food to eat. In the two days they waited for the storm to pass, Ellen was hard at work. When they set out again, Lora was surprised to see that Ellen's long gown was now breeks.

"That was quite clever, Lady Ellen."

"What do you mean, Lora?"

"Sewing your gown to make pants like the Elves wear. It's a lot easier to move around now, isn't it?"

Ellen laughed. "Yes, it is. I had enough thread to do the same for the children."

"They'll find walking easier now too. Ellen, help as many of the others to do the same thing as you can." She patted the woman on the shoulder then moved further along the line.

Later in the day she slipped ahead to hunt. An old elk was brought down and that night there was meat roasting on the fires. Some of the other Elves had successful hunts as well. Lora declared it a feast day so everybody ate their fill.

There was food and wood aplenty where they'd camped, so they stayed. This time, the Elves began to teach the women and older children how to shoot a bow.

"Before the winter is gone," said Lora as she walked among them, "you will know how to survive and thrive in the forest. You will be proficient with sword and dagger as well as with the spear and bow. Never again will you depend on another to make a safe life for you, you will do this for yourself. Never again will you depend on the generosity of the Geni."

WHILE LORA AND HER Reavers nurtured a new band of forest runners, the people at the gates of Magdan huddled together and suffered. They had no food, and little clothing that could keep the winter at bay. They'd been herded together and forced out through the gates by the men at arms, some who had families in the people who were chased from the city.

"The city seems empty now," mused one watchman.

"I know," replied his companion. "Was your family expelled as well?"

"Yes, all were forced beyond the walls. I'd have gone with them, but I didn't want to face death in mage fire. As it is, I was able to drop some food over the wall to my wife. I can do more for my family alive than I can dead."

While the two men talked they didn't see a shadowy figure scale the wall and disappear into the city. Arlaith kept to the shadows as she moved from house to house. She'd learned much since the queen had bought her from the innkeeper years before. Where before she'd been a frightened and abused girl, now she was a hardened warrior of the Bornani.

She'd traveled to Fugitive with the Orcs. During that trip Saggit had implanted the understanding of honor. By the time they'd reached the town she'd vowed to make that her life's guide. From there the Borni had taught her fighting skills, stealth, and forest survival. She learned to talk to the wind, water, and the beasts of the forest. Now she was using all her new skills.

Through much of the night she prowled the streets and alleys of Magdan. She gathered food and warm clothing, hiding it near the walls. When the dawn came she found a hiding place and slept. As darkness fell she awakened and set about her task once again. Carefully she watched the men patrolling the walls. She found the blind spot then gave the cry of the hunting hawk.

Below the walls another Elf waited, grinning. The huddled people watched, but made no sound. Suddenly a bundle dropped from above. The Elf caught it then waited. A while later another bundle fell then a soft bird call followed.

The Elf swept up the two bundles and approached the huddled women and children. "Here are cloaks and more, food as well. Gather together and use some of the cloaks for a shelter. Wait a few moments and I'll bring you wood and tinder."

"Why are you helping us?" asked one woman.

"I once served your people as slave because I had no choice, now I offer the hand of friendship of my own free will. If you'd rather not, I can give these things to another."

"No, wait, please. If I've ever wronged you, I beg forgiveness. Just tell us what you want."

"I want to keep you alive. I want you to understand that Elves are people, no more, no less than you or any other. You can't understand anything if you're dead, so I want to keep you alive."

"Are you going to make us slaves?"

"No, I wouldn't wish that fate on anyone, besides, the queen has forbidden it."

The woman nodded as she cuddled her children closer into the new cloak. "How can we help you?"

"Fight to survive. I'll bring wood now."

"Sir Elf."

"Yes?"

The woman reached a trembling hand toward him. "I'd like to accept that hand of friendship." He smiled as he gently gripped her hand for a moment. "We'll need help to learn a new way of living, but I swear me and mine will try."

"My name is Korath. I ask no more of you than that. Stay warm now, I'll go for wood."

He was true to his word. He soon returned with a bundle of wood. "How do I do this?" she asked. He chose a dry stick and showed her how to scrape off some tinder with the blade of a knife. Carefully cupping it together he struck a small piece of flint to the dagger. A spark caught the tinder, he cupped his hands around it and blew gently until it burst into flame. He then added a few small pieces of wood then winked and passed her the dagger and flint.

"Tell me your name, my new friend."

"Della, my name is Della. Korath, you've saved me and my children. You offer friendship where it was not earned nor deserved. I'll do all I can to be worthy of the friendship you offer." He smiled and patted her arm before vanishing into the gloom of darkness.

They fell asleep by the warm fire that night, a shelter of old cloaks protecting them from the wind. They awakened to find another pile of dry firewood by the cold ashes. Carefully the woman scraped some tinder and got it burning. She was grinning with delight as she built up the fire.

Behind the cold walls, while her accomplice was teaching a new friend how to make fire, Arlaith made a discovery. She'd just slipped into an empty house when something scurried away from her. She was on it in a heartbeat. They struggled for a moment then Arlaith had her victim pinned and a hand over her mouth to keep her silent. Only then did she realize the woman in her arms was weeping.

"Hush now. Make no sound and I'll relax my hold." The woman nodded so Arlaith withdrew the hand from the girl's mouth. "What are you doing here?"

"I live here. At least I did until the Geni chased my family out into the snow. My mother hid me in the cellar before they came."

"Before they came?"

"I was to be given in marriage to an old merchant, but mother hid me thinking that's who was coming to the door. However, the Watch came and chased everyone out the gates."

Arlaith realized the weeping woman was terrified, shivering from the cold, and trembling from both fear and hunger. "Here, let me squirm around a bit so I can cuddle you warm in my cloak. I've got some food to share. You hungry?"

The woman nodded eagerly and cuddled into Arlaith's arms. She hungrily attacked the cake of pressed berries that was passed to her. For some reason she couldn't name, Arlaith cuddled the young woman closer and cooed soothing sounds. "Hush now, Arlaith will keep you safe. You're safe now."

"They came beating at the door," sniffed the woman. "They killed my grandfather and dragged my mother away by the hair. They said Father had been slain by the mage because he refused to obey. Please don't let them find me." She snuggled deeper into Arlaith's embrace.

Arlaith kissed her hair and smiled. "You're warming up nicely. Here's another travel cake. Eat it now, build up your strength. So, tell me, who is this woman snuggled in my arms?"

"Julie, my name is Julie," she replied as she began to disentangle herself from Arlaith's arms.

"Oh no you don't, you get right back here and cuddle with me some more. It'll be a lot easier for us to stay warm this way." Julie eagerly snuggled closer once again.

"Why Miss Julie, I think you enjoy a cuddle."

Her reply was so soft Arlaith could barely hear it. "Yes."

"Especially with a woman?"

"Yes. Please don't kill me."

"My dear girl, why ever would I do that?"

"Father threatened to if he caught me kissing a girl again. That's why he was so eager to marry me off."

"I see. Well, Julie, I'll let you in on a small secret. I like cuddling girls too."

"Are you allowed to do that?"

"Elves choose for themselves, sweetie. The queen herself has chosen a woman as life companion."

"Well then, I wish I'd been born an Elf."

"No you don't, girl. That was no life worth living. Listen now. I was an abused slave, a serving wench at an inn. Queen Ariel was there looking for someone else, but she brought me out, and set me free. A slave's life isn't one to be envied."

"But she set you free. I wish someone would set me free."

Arlaith chuckled. "Now that I can do. We'll find you some clothes better suited to winter travel in the forest. I'll take you over the wall with me. Once free of the Geni, and living in the lands ruled by Queen Ariel, you'll be free to choose your own fate."

"Could I stay with you?" Julie's face became anxious again.

Arlaith smiled reassuringly. "Well, it would make it a lot easier to stay warm through the winter. I suppose we'll just have to see where life takes us once the snows melt. Yes, my cuddle buddy, we'll face the winter together. First thing we need to do is get you better clothes and some weapons."

Over the next two days they looted every house they could break into. Now dressed in warm leggings and heavy tunics, Julie was becoming an accomplished burglar. They threw what they found over the wall to the people below. On the third night Arlaith lowered Julie over the wall then followed her to the snow below. They'd been spotted and the Watch was searching for them. It was far too dangerous to remain in the city.

The Elves soon learned that Julie had a knack for persuasion as she talked many of the refugees into working together to survive instead of fighting among themselves. Then one day two strange Elves arrived in the night. Julie's eyes widened as all the Elves knelt before them. The queen had arrived.

The word was soon spread, a plan devised, then Arlaith was called to the queen's campfire. "Arlaith, my sister, you seem to have acquired a companion. Come closer, Julie is it?"

The girl came forward and knelt. "Yes, Lady, I'm Julie."

Ariel raised her up and patted the ground beside her. "Julie, we're going to sack the city. We're going to take everybody back inside and throw out everybody who's still in there."

Wide eyed, the girl gazed at the queen. "Do you need me to lead Elves back inside, Ar... Lady Ariel?"

"So, you know me, do you?"

"Yes, Lady. You were in the Watch and wouldn't let the men have me when I was caught out alone at night."

"Yes, I remember that. You were just a child then. I have to say, you've grown into a fine young woman.

"Now, Julie, advise me. I'm well versed in the layout of the city, but it's been some time since I was within these walls. What will I find there?"

"The poor part of town is empty now, Lady, the military family section as well. The wealthy remain in the grander houses, the men at arms and the Watch are in the barracks, all the remaining slaves are quartered in the houses of the wealthy and guarded. The Overlord and his mage are in the palace. The Watch patrols the walls and the empty houses now. The storehouses are heavily guarded as well."

"Julie and I gathered every scrap of food we could find and tossed it over the walls. Winter weight clothing as well we took," said Arlaith.

"It was well done, ladies," said Ariel. "Arlaith, spread the word, we go tonight. At the fall of darkness we enter the city."

Darkness had fallen and clouds covered the moon. What light there was came from guttering torches. The two men of the Watch walked slowly toward each, passed with a few words of complaint, then proceeded. They were several paces apart when the shadows came over the wall. Within the space of a few heartbeats, two corpses were thrown into the darkness below.

With the Watch silenced, the Elves poured into the city, two hundred strong. Silent as hunting shadows they dropped from the parapets to the empty streets. When the light of day returned, the people in the finer houses as well as the palace found the guards all dead. The alarm sounded.

Men at arms poured from the barracks but there was no apparent enemy to fight. And then a man fell, an arrow in his chest. More arrows rained down from the roof tops and more men fell. The men at arms took shelter in doorways and inside houses.

By this time panic was spreading through Magdan. Wealthy people huddled behind their personal guards, trembling in terror. In his palace the Geni overlord cursed at the cowering mage, a human who was little more than an apprentice. His seeing stone would not respond, neither he nor his Geni master could awaken it.

The Elf Queen had come, and her magic was more powerful than they could have imagined. The Geni stopped cursing and making threats as they heard a clear ringing voice. That voice, magically enhanced, could be heard throughout the city and beyond its walls.

"People of Magdan, hear my words. I am Ariel, Queen of the Elves. I've come with a twofold purpose. I've come to free the slaves, and to expel the Geni. Bring them out into the streets now if you want to survive. Do it quickly for I grow impatient."

Ariel didn't have long to wait. Soon after she spoke a door opened and a Geni, bound hand and foot was thrust out into the street. Two more, three young, and a half dozen finely dressed females followed at sword point. Eight slaves as well followed and stood shivering in the cold.

Two Elvish warriors approached the armed guards that held the swords. "Is this all from that house?"

"It is," replied one man.

The Elf turned to one of the slaves. "Does he speak the truth?"

"Yes, master. The house is empty now."

"I'm not your master, I'm a friend. My name is Tanis. Go back inside now and build up the fire, stay warm. Eat your fill, gather warmer clothing, and dress yourselves in it. We'll return for you soon." He smiled and patted the woman's shoulder.

"You men at arms, take your prisoners to the gates. Archers will be watching from above."

They marched away and he moved on to another house where people had come forth. This time it was a rich Orc and his family. The Orc challenged him, and Tanis slew him easily. Again the armed guards led their captives to the gates while the former slaves were sent back inside to keep warm.

The next house was a different story. As Tanis approached there was a sudden rush of armed men. A hail of arrows from above brought down a few, but their heavy armor protected them for the most part. That did them little good as they found the Elves to be highly skilled warriors, not simple rebellious slaves as they'd imagined.

In short order Tanis, Korath, and the rest of the Queen's Guard stood amid the blood, corpses, and carnage they'd wrought. Eighteen men at arms lay dead and only one Elf had taken a wound. The Elves poured through the now open door. Screams echoed from inside, then a number of people were herded out bitter winter air.

That scene was repeated over and over as some of the men at arms revolted and drove their former employers out, and others tried to mount a defense. At the end, over five hundred people were herded out through the gates, guarded by their former men at arms and Ariel's Elves. A hundred and ten slaves were set free that day as well.

In the palace of the overlord, things had gone awry quickly. The Geni overlord trembled in fear as he saw the mage go blind then fall slowly to the floor, dead. He swallowed hard and braced his back against the wall as he listened to the soft footfalls in the corridor, pacing slowly towards the chamber of audience where he huddled in fear by the fire.

A female Elf in mage's robes strode into the room. "I am Trelanzh. I killed your mage, as I did so many others of your kind at the breaking of the world. Go outside now and join your people or die where you stand."

He fled outside and, shivering in the cold, tried to hide himself in the group. He failed. An old Elf wearing the colors of the Queen's Guard stepped into the group and felled him with a single blow. The Geni was dragged out into the open then thrust away. "Do you remember me, Geni?"

"No," was the fearful answer as the former overlord cowered away from the Elf.

"I remember you. My name is Olan." With that the Elf leaped at the Geni and thrust a sword through his heart.

Korath stepped up and gripped the old Elf by the shoulder. "Take the others to the gates now, old friend." Olan nodded and began herding the other captives away.

The gates were opened and the people of Magdan herded out through into the winter's cold. The Elves marched them well away from the gates, then the Queen's voice, magically enhanced, was heard again.

"Hear me, people of Magdan. Inside these walls are a hundred former slaves. They, accompanied by a number of my warriors, will remain within the city to wait out the winter.

"Those of you who were forced from the gates by your own people are welcome to go back inside and return to your homes. So are the refugees from the summer wars. The Elves will help you loot the homes and storehouses of the wealthy so you may pass the winter in comfort.

"Be warned. When the snows leave the lands the Elves will burn Magdan to the ground. There are several destroyed villages near here and you are welcome to rebuild them. We will help you, but know this, Elves are not slaves. We are a free people. We offer the hand of friendship to those who are willing to accept it.

"Those of you who cannot live with free Elves among you will join the Geni on their journey south or remain and be hunted down and killed. That choice is yours to make.

"So, the gates are open. Go inside now, our new friends. Get yourselves home and warm."

There was a sudden rush of the people from the gates who'd been forced out. In short order they were back inside hurrying to the shelter of their homes. When they were all inside, as well as the refugees from before, Ariel spoke again.

"You men at arms, those of you would return to your families, lay down your weapons and return to the city. Those of you who prefer the company of the Geni will travel with them." All but a half dozen men dropped their swords and shields then trooped back through the city gates.

"The lands of the Geni are to the south," Ariel continued. "That is your road, both Geni and the rest of you. Go there and you will not be hindered. Vary from that path and you will be hunted."

"We have no food to means of travel," shouted one Geni. "We'll all freeze to death."

"A fate you so recently forced upon others. Move on or die where you stand."

"What about us," cried one woman. She was richly dressed, and Ariel knew her. "We're not Geni. Please, let us go home."

"You were favored of the Geni, lived off the labor of slaves, and hoarded the resources for yourselves. You were among those who forced the poor and families of the warriors out into the cold. That fate is now your own.

"Close the gates."

The formerly wealthy friends of the Geni overlords watched in horror as the gates swung closed and the Elves melted into the forest, vanishing from sight. Darkness fell, and with it came a chilling cutting wind from the north.

WELL BACK IN THE FOREST, in a glade sheltered from the north winds, the queen sat with her Elves beside a warm fire.

"My queen, they won't last three days, you know this," Mearith said without looking up from the fire.

"I know," was the soft reply.

"It's tempting, isn't it?"

"Mearith?"

"To let them suffer and die, a fate they and their kind foisted on your people for centuries. My delight, I know you. If you do this you will be tormented."

Ariel sighed and looked to the darkened sky. "I'm already tormented, my heart. Every instinct I have tells me to find them and blast them into oblivion. To send Tanis and his Reavers against them. If they reach the lands of the south they could marshal the wild tribes and return to make war upon us."

"But?"

"But if I slay them outright I become them. I see why your brother Evanseth wants to pass the crown of the Borni to another, why you won't take it up."

Mearith didn't reply, she just put her arm around Ariel's shoulders. The queen poked at the fire for a moment then raised her head. "I guess there's no hope for it. All right my friends, advise me. Tanis?"

"Lady, my heart says leave them to their fate. You gave them a chance to survive."

"But?"

"But, as you say, that would make us no better than the Geni."

"And we do strive to be better than the Geni," agreed Ariel. "So, we're agreed, we don't let them starve. I'm open to suggestions. Trelanth?"

"Well, we can't let them return to Magdan, especially the Geni, nor would I want to. I suppose what we need is a place for them to pass the rest of the winter, a place where they can survive if they work at it."

"Work at it," grinned Korath. "That'll be a novel concept for them. None of those people has managed an hour of actual work in their entire lives."

Ariel's eyes brightened at that. "Agreed, Korath. I believe it's time they learned. Tanis, send a runner to Mexah, tell him I need a dozen of his warriors for a special mission.

"Here's what I propose. There's an empty village about four days march for these people, perhaps five. There're a few buildings still standing. We'll help them as little as possible to reach that shelter, but we will help them. Once there they'll have to search the ground for food, find and retrieve firewood, etc. The dozen Elves will do the minimum to ensure their survival.

"When the snows leave the lands, the Geni will continue their journey south, but the humans and Orcs may choose to remain in that village and make a life for themselves there. If they choose to do that and accept Elves as a free people we will help them, if not, they join the Geni on the road.

"What think you, my heart? This much I can do, but I cannot bring myself to help them as we do the others."

"I think it's a fine compromise, my delight. I like it."

"Trelanth?"

"I like it, my queen."

"Tanis?" He just nodded, but didn't speak. "Tanis, speak to me, dear friend. What is it?"

He sighed and continued to stare into the fire. "My Queen, I struggle within myself. Standing face to face with the woman who ordered the death of my mother caused a rage to swell up inside me, a rage that threatened to take me over, cause me to kill them all. It still burns inside me. Lady, I know your solution is the best, I do."

The queen reached out to gently squeeze his shoulder. "I understand, Tanis, I do. No Borni can truly understand, but I do. I won't ask you to aid your former master, Tanis. I recognized him in the group, I assume his woman gave that order. When the dawn comes, return to Magdan, ensure that all is well there, then return to Argar. Send that runner and then Mexah can deal with this."

"Thank you, my queen. I know I need to control the rage within, but seeing her face ..."

"I know, dear friend, I know. Rest now."

Tanis raised his arm and an Elf appeared at his side instantly. Tanis gave him the message and he vanished into the night. Once again Mearith spoke. "Tanis, my friend, be at peace. You're far stronger than you realize."

"Lady?"

"This past day you stood face to face with that you hate most, yet you held yourself in check. That was a feat worthy of the mightiest warrior. Mastery of the self is the hardest battle. Trust me, this I know all too well. I'm quite proud of you, my Lord Tanis." She punched his shoulder lightly. "Drakkat said you'd make a fine Orc, but I think you'd make a fine Borni as well. Rest now, the day returns soon."

Tanis smiled her then settled down and pulled his hood over his eyes. As his breathing deepened Mearith signaled Ariel and they slipped away a few paces to talk softly.

"I wish there was some way to help him," sighed Ariel.

"There is, my delight."

"Oh?"

"Recall Eline to her post as his second as soon as possible."

"Eline? I sent her with... oh dear, you mean...?"

"The poor man is lost without her, and I noticed a hint of disappointment in her eyes when ..."

"I sent her away from him. And now she's trapped in the mountains. Well, I can't make the snows melt in the high passes or my companion will frown at me for overuse of the magic, so I'll have to do the next best thing." She signaled for Trelanth.

"My queen?"

"Contact Ethor. Tell him I want Eline and her troops at Argar as soon as possible."

"My Lord Tanis will be well pleased to hear that, my queen."

"That's the idea," sighed Ariel.

"Lady, with your power, you could easily raise a portal."

"I could, Trelanth, but I have the sense those troops need to be right where they are for the winter."

"Yes, my queen. I'll contact him at once."

Back in Magdan something unusual was happening, and the Elves slowly stepped back to watch. With Arlaith at her side, and the understanding of Elvish authority behind her, Julie had taken command, but in a most unusual way. Without seeming to give a single order, she nonetheless organized the people who had rushed back inside.

Using her almost magical power of persuasion, she had Arlaith organizing the Elves as well. Within a turning of the glass from when the gates closed they had the storehouses open and were rationing out the food and clothing supplies.

Tanis arrived back at the city and marveled at how orderly things were going. There were long lines formed before the storehouses, but everybody was waiting patiently for their turn. Another line led to a fine house that had been converted to an infirmary. Arlaith approached Tanis as he stood watching.

"My Lord Tanis."

"Arlaith, what mage have you set to work here? I fully expected to find riots, a few fights for resources at least. How has this been managed?"

"This is the work of my sweet Julie, my lord. I know not how she does it, but I swear, she can talk anyone into anything. While outside the gates she had them all banding together for protection and shelter. Now she's got them all helping each other instead of fighting among themselves."

Tanis grinned as he watched the proceedings for a while then he spoke again. "Arlaith, I know the queen has said she'd send you and Julie to Fugitive, but I have another idea."

"Oh?"

"Grace isn't a young woman, and Argar is growing fast. Julie's skills could be a big help to her and to us as well."

"To us, my Lord?"

"When the other people see you and Julie together then see her moving about the town, bringing peace and order wherever she goes, they will more readily accept the Elves as equals. If you agree I'll speak to Queen Ariel about this and ask to keep you two with me at Argar."

Arlaith laughed with delight. "As you wish, my Lord Tanis. I'd be delighted to remain at Argar with you."

"Then I'll leave you in command of the garrison here for now. When the snows leave the land bring the people out and burn the city to the ground. This hateful place will vanish from the memory of the world."

"You were held slave here even as was Lady Ariel, yes?"

"I was, as were so many more of the Bornani."

"Then it's only fitting it be destroyed and the forest be encouraged to reclaim the place where it once stood. It shall be as you desire, my Lord." With that he strode away.

"What's going on, Arlaith?" asked Julie as she approached her lover. "Lord Tanis just told those warriors that you're in command here."

"Actually, I think he wants you to be in command," grinned Arlaith.

"Me?"

"You. Sweet Julie, you have a talent for organizing people, and for convincing them to work together. Lord Tanis wants us to remain here until the spring then lead these people out to where they can build new homes, establish new villages, resurrect the destroyed farms. He wants this city burned to the ground. He then wants us to join him at Argar."

"Why?"

"My sweet darling girl, Lord Tanis has seen your potential, and he wants you to help the headman at Argar. Her name is Grace."

Julie stepped into Arlaith's arms and snuggled into the cloak with her. "Arlaith, it scares me some days. I was terrified and hiding from the Watch, expecting to be caught, raped, and forced into marriage to that hideous old man. I'm just a scared little mouse and you make me do scary things."

"Scary things?"

"Scary things. I know what you're doing; you've done it from the first. You make me take charge, take chances, yet you're always there to help me. Now you want me to help this village headman? I can see where this is going. Before long you scary Elves will make me the headman."

"Sweetie, you're such a natural organizer. You'd be great."

"Promise you'll always stay with me and protect me?"

"I promise. Back to work now, I see a brawl about to start."

"How can you always tell?"

"I was a serving wench at an inn before I was set free. I can tell when a fight is about to start. Go on, you're the one in command here now."

"Me? You're the one in command."

"That's just what you want me to believe. I know you too well, Lady Julie. Go on now, I'll be the fearsome Elf who stands beside you to enforce your will on the rebellious public." Julie was still giggling as they reached the two arguing men.

Forest Runners

A full moon cycle had passed in the mountains as well as the forests below. Lora had gotten a report from the Gates of Shotar and many of those left behind had frozen to death, others had fallen to disease. She was pleasantly surprised at the families they'd led away from those gates. Those she'd brought away had managed to survive and as they learned the ways of the forest, were beginning to grow stronger.

One man was drawing her attention, an Elf. One of the Bornani had taken an interest in one human woman and her children. He pushed her hard, and he wasn't gentle about it. It was reaching the point where Lora was going to speak to him, assign him to another family. A glance across the camp showed him talking to her again, stepping closer to her as he spoke. As Lora neared them, she stopped to listen. The man was smiling.

"Mary, you astound me," said the Bornani.

"Why is that, Tek?"

"I've pushed you hard, you and your daughter. I've bullied you, cursed you, and was an arrogant ass at every turn."

"Yes you have been. Giving me back some of my own medicine, I expect. That would be hard to resist."

"Yes it was, but that's not why I did it."

"Oh?"

"You were a far less harsh master than many I could have served, Mary" said Tek. "I want you and your children to survive, but I'm

81

damned if I'll do it for you. I pushed you hard and, to my surprise, you've risen to the challenge. Of all these people, you've taken to the bow faster, and are a better shot than any of them. You work hard at gathering wood for the fire, and you constantly search the ground for edibles, nuts, dried berries, and more.

"As a result, you've grown strong again, and so have your children. We still have a few cycles of the moon to go, but when the warmth returns to the lands you'll be ready. You'll survive, Mary, and so will your children. Better yet, you won't have to depend on anyone else for it, not a man, Geni, nor and Elf. I'm actually quite proud of you."

"So, does this mean you'll stop bullying me?" asked Mary, a twinkle in her eye.

He laughed with delight to see her grin. "It does. I once overheard the queen say that people need to learn to accept Elves as equals, that we need to build friendships with the other races if we can. So, for years you bullied and cursed at me, and now I have repaid you in kind. Can we now set all that aside and be friends?"

"Friends? You want to be friends?"

"Yes I do," he grinned as he held out his hand.

She laughed as she accepted his hand in hers. "All right, but the next time you curse at me I'll shoot you in the butt with an arrow."

"Duly warned," he grinned. "Rest well this night, Mary. Tomorrow you and I will hunt together as friends and fellow hunters. We'll bring back meat enough for several families." She had a bemused smile on her face as he walked away.

Lora stepped into Tek's path as he crossed the camp. "You and Mary hunting together? You gave her the hand of friendship?"

"I was hard on her because she needed to find her strength. All her life she's taken the easy path, Elf do this, slave do that, Father help me here, Husband, take care of that for me. She used her beauty and wits to get along, but no more. That didn't work here, not with me. Now she's found her strength, her independence, and is starting to enjoy it."

"I'm curious, Tek. She was your master, why go to the effort for her?"

"In all the years I served her family she never once allowed them to beat us. Not once did I feel the whip because of her. I owed her this and more."

"Tek, I apologize, for I've wronged you. I should have consulted you sooner, instead I came to rebuke you."

"Accepted, Lora of the Borni. Friends?"

Lora took his hand in hers. "Friends, Tek of the Bornani." She slapped his shoulder then walked away, seeking out Ellen and Garret. She found them sharing a fire with several other families. There was venison on the spit and laughter in the air.

"Ho, friends of the Elves, what are we celebrating?"

"Lora, join us," said Garret. "We're celebrating Ellen's first kill. She brought down the deer with a single arrow. She then made me carry it back to camp."

"Of course I did," smiled Ellen. "What's the point of having a man at arms if he won't carry the meat for you? Right, Lora?"

"Absolutely right, Lady Ellen," grinned Lora. "So, all is well here?"

"It is, Lady," said one of the other women. "Ellen and Garret hunted, others of us gathered firewood, searched out caches of nuts, found a few open spaces and gleaned a few roots for the stew pot."

"I have to say, I'm extremely proud of you all," said Lora. "Feast and enjoy, my friends."

She patted Ellen on the shoulder as she moved to the next fire. She grew more impressed as she made her way through the entire encampment. Everywhere she found it the same, they'd formed themselves into groups. They took turns hunting and gathering and everybody seemed to be gaining strength and confidence.

It was late in the night when the alarm sounded. The camp was suddenly filled with screams of terror, howls of insane rage, war cries, and sounds of battle. Savage wolf-like creatures ravaged through the camp.

Arrows flew like raindrops and the marauders fell, blood on their fangs and arrows in their hearts. The attack had come suddenly, but the Elves had responded instantly. Lora ran past Garret and Ellen who stood back to back, defending their children. The bodies of three attackers gave testament to their success.

The battle was over by the time the light of dawn reached the forest camp. Lora nodded her approval as she saw several women pulling arrows from the bodies of the dead creatures. The Elves then threw the carcasses into the trees away from the camp.

The lone healer was busy with the injured, three of the women assisting him. The keening of the bereaved filled the air as mothers and elders clutched the bodies of the dead, many children, to them, rocking back and forth inconsolably.

"Lora."

"How many Elves did we lose, Tek?"

"One, six wounds, none fatal."

"The humans and Orcs?"

"Eighteen dead, over thirty wounds, nine probably fatal. It's as though the beasts sensed which ones were the weakest."

"Where did they come from? Who's guard post did they attack?"

"Roga's, he's dead," sighed Tek. "They came in a rush, late in the night. He gave the alarm and fought them, but they were too many."

"We need a better encampment, something easier to defend," said Lora.

"I'll scout ahead."

"Tek, take someone with you." He nodded as he trotted away. She watched as he stopped to check in with Mary, then left the camp with a Borni warrior at his side. Lora nodded her approval then sought out Ellen and Garret.

That day they remained in camp. The Elves gathered firewood, leaving the humans and Orcs to mourn their dead. At night the watch was tripled, and no one stood alone. Three days in all they stayed that way while they performed ceremonies for the departed, and then Lora moved them on.

"Forgive me, my people, but we must move the camp. The winter is still cold, and we need food and fire."

Tek returned at high sun. "There's a wide but shallow cavern ahead, Lora. The overhanging rock will protect from rain and snow as well as break the wind. With that wall of stone at our back it will be harder for an enemy to get at us."

"Can we reach it before darkness?"

"No, another day at best speed for the elders and children."

Lora nodded slowly. "Then we'll go slow. We have wounded and bereaved with us as well as elders and youngsters. Rest now, my friend. We'll double the watch this night."

The next day they reached the shallow cavern. It was well protected and perfect for their needs. They swiftly set up camp then rested for the night. Again the watch was doubled.

At dawn they returned to the ways of hunting and gathering, archery practice, and now weapons training was added. If they were to face unnatural enemies in the forest they needed to develop some fighting skills.

Over the ensuing days Lora noticed something interesting. Among the humans and Orcs three people seemed to rise to leadership roles, Mary, Ellen, and Garret. Mary especially had a knack for organizing and people slowly began to look to her for direction.

While Mary began to take over the organizing of the hunters, Ellen began to direct the work of the camp, gathering of firewood, and whatever could be eaten. Garret began to teach them to fight and defend as a unified troop. Slowly but surely, the humans and Orcs were becoming independent from the Elves.

As a result of this Lora and the Elves began a new task. They spread out through the forest, searching for anything that might threaten the new community of people forming at the cavern. They found and eliminated another small band of the wolf creatures and a wandering monster, something that looked like an Ogre crossed with a demon. It put up one hell of a fight, but they brought it down.

After another week Lora believed the refugees to be somewhat self-sufficient. She took half her hundred warriors and left the remaining fifty with Tek to guard and help the new forest runners. She went back to the Gates of Shotar.

WHILE THE QUEEN TOOK Magdan once again, and Lora created a few hundred new forest runners, Eline grew bored in the fastness of the mountains. She responded quickly as the alarm sounded. A band of wolf creatures had approached the way station. The two hundred Elves camped there made short work of them, yet Ethor was troubled.

"Eline, look at this."

"The beasts wear armor and carry trophies of their kills. That's disturbing. Ethor, I doubt we'll be able to make allies out of these creatures, even if they become a people."

"Understood and agreed. What I'm seeing is a Dwarf child's hand, an Elf's ear, and a human scrotum."

"Yes, and this one has more. An Orc's tusk, and a Coti scalp."

"Yes, I see more Coti trophies, fresh trophies."

"Worried about your girlfriend?"

"Woman, I've warned you about this before..." Eline's mischievous laughter broke his somber mood. "Yes, I'll admit I'm concerned for Kekka and her people."

"Come, Ethor, stop this and look to her village, see how they're managing the winter. Take up your scrying crystal now. I'll stand the watch for you."

Ethor nodded and fetched his pack, taking out the crystal and settling down beside the fire. Eline stood near, motioning anyone who approached to move away. A long time later she heard him sigh and put away the seeing stone.

"Well?"

"It's not good, Eline. They were raided by some sort of monsters just at harvest time. Most of their crops were ruined. Their food's run out, and, with all their males dead, Kekka has led a few females out to hunt. She's tried to fix the knife I gave her to a spear. I believe they're headed this way, but I can't be certain."

"Then we'll watch for them."

Two days later the alarm was sounded again. Eline went running to find a small band of the Coti surrounded by Elvish archers. They'd been told not to kill unless they had no choice. Eline approached with her arms spread wide, her hands empty. "Kekka?"

The big female with the spear turned to her instantly. She slapped her chest. "Kekka." She then swept out her arm to indicate the Elvish encampment. "Etor?"

Eline grinned her delight. "Someone fetch Ethor for me." She turned to the Coti woman again and patted her own chest. "Eline. Friend Ethor. Friend Kekka?"

The woman dropped her spear and barked an order. The others also dropped their crude weapons. "Eeeline friend Etor, friend Kekka."

"They're friendly. Go get some food on the fire, we have guests." The Elvish archers lowered their bows and trotted back to the way station. Eline motioned with her arm. "Kekka, come, food. All come, food." She turned her back and walked away. Kekka grunted an order, picked up her spear and followed.

Ethor met them halfway to the station. He greeted Kekka warmly then joined the escort leading the Coti to the warmth of the fires. The dozen Coti females were fed until they could eat no more. Only then did Ethor engage Kekka in conversation. "Kekka full?"

"Full," she replied, patting her belly. "Food good."

"Food gone at home?"

She thought for a moment until she was certain she understood the question. "Bad things come. Kill people. Ruin crops. Food gone. People starve. Stupid mage, take men, fight Elf. All kill. No men fight monster."

Many of the Elves heard this and they knew, although they'd had no choice, they'd still been the cause of these people's suffering. Eline made eye contact with several and knew they agreed. They had to do something to help the Coti. She and Ethor exchanged glances and she nodded.

Ethor looked to Kekka. "More Coti back home?"

She nodded. "Old, young, no hunt. Hungry."

"Kekka, people live better in trees?" She tilted her head, trying to understand his question so he tried again. "Trees here. Trees make better shelter. Some food grow on trees. Some food hide in trees. Plenty water here. Better soil. Grow more food here in trees. This better place for Kekka people?"

Slowly the light of understanding reached her eyes. "This good place. Kekka bring all Coti here? Elf share food? No kill?"

"Elf share food. Share land. No kill. Elf friend Kekka people."

She was somewhat overcome and took a moment to gather her emotions. This was so much more than she'd hoped for. In truth all she'd dare hope for was permission to hunt. "Kekka Coti come here? Live always?"

Ethor grinned as he replied. "Kekka Coti come here. Live always. Elf help."

She made a gesture with her hand, touching her heart then sweeping her hand out to encompass the Elves. "Kekka, Coti, grateful. Try help Elf too. Friends."

"Kekka Coti, Elf, friends," said Ethor, nodding his agreement.

"Elf help Coti, save life. How Coti help Elf?"

Ethor tapped his forehead. "Coti smart. Coti know path through mountains. Coti teach Elf trails through mountains?"

She nodded eagerly, happy to be able to repay some of the kindress these folk offered. Kekka turned and jabbered at her companions, filling them in on what had been discussed. They were amazed, delighted, astounded, and more. They were to be allowed to come down out of the mountains and live in the forest again.

With all these savage Elves to protect them they would be safe; their young would survive. When they realized they would have to help the Elves find the hidden pathways through the mountains they became wary. However, Kekka pointed out their young and elders would soon perish in the cold without food, they readily agreed. The bargain was sealed.

They rested in the way station that night then the next morning they set out for home, a dozen Elves with sacks of food accompanying them. A week later they were back at the way station. The Elves set them up in a few shelters near the trees and river. They brought them food and firewood.

Soon the Coti were foraging in the forest again. Each time they were escorted by armed Elves. It was good that it happened this way. On one trip they encountered a small pack of wolf creatures. The Coti females stood together trembling, but the Elves quickly dispatched the maddened attackers. Not one Coti had taken an injury. After that they willingly accepted the Elvish escorts.

Kekka's grasp of the common language grew rapidly, and she sat in conversation with the Elves every chance she got. Slowly the Elves learned of the fate of her people. The men had fallen under the spell of the Stupid Mage, as she called the evil one Trelanth had killed.

Every male from her village had been killed in that war. "Stupid Mage, stupid men. They should have stayed home. Hunt, work, grow food, defend village." Of a village over two hundred strong, barely forty Coti had survived to reach the way station and the protection of the

Elves. They all knew that without Kekka making friends with Ethor the Elf, none would have survived the winter.

After a couple of weeks, Eline approached Kekka with an idea. When the snows were gone she wanted Kekka to go with some of the Elves to other Coti villages, tell them her story, help the Elves make friends of all the Coti. She readily agreed.

"IT APPEARS WE HAVE new allies in the mountains, Lady Ariel."

"Trelanth?"

"Eline's just taken in all that remains of the Coti village Ethor claimed as friendly, my queen. They must have fallen on further hard times as barely forty of them survived to reach the way station. Ethor says their leader, his friend Kekka, has agreed to go to the other Coti villages, tell her story, try to make allies of them."

"He believes this is possible?"

"He does, Lady. The key is the forest."

"Explain."

"The Coti were creatures of the forest, but driven into the hard places of the mountains by hunters. Ethor has invited Kekka and her small clan to live in the forest near the way station. He believes that, if the Elves prevent the Coti from being hunted, accepting them back into the forest, we will gain their trust and aid as mountain guides and lookouts."

"By all the power," said Mearith as she poked at the fire and tossed on another stick. "Trelanth, we owe you much."

"Lady Mearith?"

"You prevented Tanis from destroying those people. Ethor then, by a simple act of kindness, set in motion a series of events that could play a mighty role in this war."

"Even more," said Ariel.

"My delight?"

"Look at how the Bornani change as they are freed and nurtured by the Borni. They grow stronger, become greater than they were. I suspect it will be the same for the Coti. I think that, as allies and friends of the Elves, they will make a sudden leap towards becoming more as a people."

"I believe you're right, my delight. I wish I could be there to see it happen."

"As do I, but we have other errands. Trelanth, as the light returns to the world, take the rest of your warriors and return to Tanis at Argar. We will await the coming of Mexah's fighters."

"My delight..."

"I know, my heart, I know. When Trelanth departs for Argar we will approach the Geni. We have not the time to wait for the others to arrive."

THE NUMBERS OF THE Geni and their wealthy supporters huddled beside the fires built up by the few men at arms who had accompanied them. A few of the Orcs and humans had grudgingly begun to gather fuel for the fires, but they were growing weak from hunger. A dozen had already succumbed to the cold.

As the morning sun rose over the nearby trees they saw a group of people approaching. They huddled closer together as it became apparent it was the Elf Queen and her personal guard. "Have you come to murder us all?" demanded one Geni female. "Does the cold not work fast enough for your revenge?"

"If revenge was my desire you would all have perished in torment before now." Ariel's voice was harsh and unforgiving. She waved her hand and the campfires leaped up, the flames roaring, the heat driving the Geni back.

Ariel lowered her arm and the fires returned to normal. "I have come to offer you a chance at life. Near this place is a small village, burned out by my warriors. There are a couple of sheds and barns still standing.

"You can shelter there for the winter, however you'll have to search the forests and fields for firewood and edible things to sustain you. I'll lead you there and detail warriors to watch you. They'll help you survive, but no more than that. They will not be your servants, rather they will be your jailers.

"So that's the alternative to a cold death in the snows. The days will be long and hard, you will be cold, hungry, and you will survive by your own efforts, or you will perish. Choose now."

One of the men at arms stepped forward. "We accept your offer. It's more than we had a right to expect. Lead on. Those who don't follow deserve to die in the snows anyway."

Without another word Ariel turned and walked away. A glance back told her the entire group was following as best they could. At the top of a small rise she stopped and held out her arm, pointing to a few scattered buildings, huddled in a shallow valley. The man at arms nodded and led the way down into that valley, the rest of the rag tag refugees following his steps through the snow.

The Elves watched from the rise as they spread out to overfill the few standing buildings. They could hear the voice of that man at arms as he bellowed directions. "Fires outside only for now. This is all the shelter we have, don't burn it down. Some of you start searching the drifts for burnable wood. Others search for fallen homes or downed storage bins hidden in the snows."

"What do you think, Mearith my heart?"

"I think that man will manage to keep quite a few of them alive. I expect that, by the time the snows leave the lands a number of them will elect to remain and build up homes here, the rest will go south."

"Then we've done what we must. Here come Mexah's warriors. We'll let them know what we're trying to do then we'll head out to see what Mexah himself is up to."

"Sounds like fun to me," grinned Mearith.

Making it Work

While the queen delivered the Geni to their possible safe haven, Rakka was trying to settle into her new role, a role she'd never expected to have in this lifetime.

"What's on your mind, my new sister?" asked Freida as she continued to work the metal. Her powerful muscles gleaming in the heat of the forge as she swung the hammer.

"I confess, I feel like such a fraud."

"Oh?"

"I've never dreamed of so high a station. I spent my life just trying to survive. I accepted a man at arms because they and their families were fed regularly. That didn't last long, for he didn't return from these walls, and I was forced out into the snow with a young child and an elderly father."

"And now you're a chieftain's mate," grinned Freida, "and you're expected to organize and command the families as your mate does the warriors."

"Yes, and I have no idea at all how to do that properly."

"Does it matter?"

"It does, Lady Blacksmith, it truly does. I want to bring honor to my chieftain and our clan. How can I be worthy of Drakkat as mate, or you as a friend, if I just ignore my responsibilities, or if I do it with half a heart?"

Frieda smiled and turned the metal over on the anvil then struck it a mighty blow. "You could be overlooking something."

"Oh?"

"Ariel is queen of the Elves, yet, when she has a decision to make, she calls those whose opinion she values to advise her. Once they help her devise a plan of action, she then designates someone to make certain it gets done. She doesn't try to do everything herself."

Rakka looked thoughtful for a moment. "So, you think I should consult Saggit's mate?"

"She was once a chieftain's mate, she knows the role well."

"I'm afraid to, what if she's angry that I've taken the authority from her?"

"She's not."

"Are you so certain?"

"If she was would she have worked so hard to force Drakkat to choose a mate?"

"If you look at it that way, I guess she wouldn't have. So, you think I should seek her advice?"

"I do, yes," said Freida as she laid aside her hammer and turned to gently grip Rakka by the shoulders. "My new sister, you need advisers, Orc women who can help you. Remember, all want to survive and thrive. Every woman in the clan wants the clan to grow stronger, more prosperous. Go to them, ask their advice.

"Kreen will be a great asset for you, choose an older woman as well, for she will have a lifetime of experience to draw upon. Choose a young one also, for the needs of the young must be considered also. Go now, my sister, go forth and conquer."

"Whatever did I do for the gods to bless me with such a friend as you?"

Freida laughed and gave her shoulders a squeeze. "Go on now, go play with your new clan. I have work to do."

With a laugh of delight Rakka fled the forge and headed back to the Orc village. Her first stop was Kreen's house. She found her alone. "Welcome, Rakka, my poor house is honored by your visit."

"Gods, I wish I could do that," sighed Rakka as she kicked off her boots and sat to the fire.

"Do what?"

"Put people at ease so quickly, make every one of them feel special and valued."

Kreen didn't speak for a moment. "Why have you sought me out, Rakka?"

"I need your help, Kreen," replied Rakka, blushing shyly. "You know well the ways and manners of a chieftain's mate. I do not. Will you teach me, help me to bring honor to the chieftain and the clan."

Kreen's face split into a warm smile. "I'm honored to be asked, Rakka, and yes, I'll do all in my power to help you. At first I thought you might not come, for I sensed a distance from you."

Rakka looked at the powerful woman and lowered her eyes, then threw back her head and laughed. "You scare the hell out of me, Kreen. I was afraid to ask for your help for fear you might eat me alive."

"You weren't certain you could trust me. What changed your mind?"

"Princess Freida. I was bemoaning my fate and fears to her this day. She said I should come to you for help."

Kreen smiled her surprise and delight. The blacksmith had given no previous indication that she had noticed Kreen's efforts to help the clan. Apparently, she had. "I must thank her for her confidence in me when next we meet. What else did she say?"

"She said first to ask your help, then bring two others into my confidence, an elder and a young one just approaching her years as a woman of the clan."

"Did she now? There is more to the Lady Blacksmith than meets the eye."

"Aye, indeed there is. So, who do we consult?"

"About what?"

"Everything. Dammit, Kreen, I'm of a poor and now dead clan. I've never even dreamed of rising so high, and I have no idea at all what to do next."

Kreen chuckled at that. "I will, my new sister. It's winter now, not so much to do except keep down the squabbles."

"I'd like to do more."

"Oh? Tell me, what more would you do? What would you have of the women of your clan?"

"There are strange things in the forest. They attacked us on the way here and I fought them beside my chieftain and my friend the blacksmith. If those things attack here the clan will be the first to feel their bite."

"So?"

"So I'd like us to work on our fighting skills, not just as individuals, but as a group, a clan. We'd need to put our backs together, the children inside that circle, and elders with bows... You're laughing at me."

"Yes I am, laughing with delight to see you're the right woman for the job. Drakkat has chosen well. You're absolutely right, Rakka. That's exactly what we must do, but I found resistance, as I wasn't the chieftain's mate. I don't have the authority to enforce this, you do."

"So why didn't you tell me?"

"Had I approached you with a 'Here's what we have to do' attitude you'd have skewered me with that pretty sword the princess gave you. You needed to arrive at the decision yourself."

"Well from now on, if you see something that needs to be done, tell me. I promise to keep the sword in its scabbard.

"Now, tell me what else I must do, and what I've neglected."

"You need to meet your people, Rakka. Go to each house, introduce yourself, talk to, and listen to, each woman you meet. Let them know they can approach you if needs be."

"Will you come with me?"

"I will. That way everyone will see that we're together on this, that there will be no competition between us. You're the chieftain's mate, I'm your friend and helper. We'll knit this clan together tighter than an old Geni's purse strings."

Rakka's sudden laughter made Kreen chuckle with delight. "Come, my new sister, let's be about the business."

"SO, I HEAR YOU'VE GOT the entire clan training like a military force," said Freida as she tapped gently at the metal on the anvil, gently shaping it into form.

"Kreen tried to make me think it was my idea, but she's the one who thought of it. You were quite right, I needed her help, and I owe you for making me go to her."

Freida grinned and kept tapping at the piece of work before her. "I heard drums last night as well."

"Yes, the young ones need ways to burn off excess energy. Nell thought dancing might be good. I've got to admit, she was right."

"And what of the elders?"

"We meet to work on leather and cloth, the elders teaching the skills as well as telling the stories of clans gone by. This is how we learn our history, and from there we can decide where we want to go in the days to come.

"You knew all this would happen didn't you, Lady Freida?"

"No, but I hoped. Hoped you'd find your way, and thereby find your place, your peace of heart."

Suddenly Rakka's eyes opened wide. "This is that place for you, isn't it? This forge is your anchor, like the hearthstone is for the clan. This is where you find your peace of heart, and why you're so loathe to leave it." Freida gave her a shy smile and nodded.

"Then I'll make my clan stronger, so strong no invader will ever get close to this forge. This forge is now sacred ground for the Scraitite Clan. I swear it on my honor."

Freida gave her a shy smile then put her arm around the woman's shoulders. "Come, my friend, let's away to the inn and see what's in the cooking pot. I'll stand you a pint." They walked to the inn arm in arm.

WHILE THE PRINCESS Freida treated her friend to a pint and a meal at the inn, Ethor brought Eline some welcome news. "Eline."

"Ethor, what brings that smile of delight to your face this snowy day?"

"I have news, and a royal command for you."

"Truly? Sit to the fire with me then, tell me all."

Grinning, he sat beside the fire tossed another stick on it. "First, the city of Magdan has fallen."

"Fallen? So soon?"

"Yes. The Geni decided to save resources by expelling all the poor as well as the families of their fighting men. They did this in all the cities. Lady Ariel was near Magdan at the time, and since it was already weakened by her attack last year, they took it again, expelled the Geni, the wealthy supporters of the Geni, and the men at arms. They brought the poor and the families back inside to pass the winter in comfort. When the snows leave the lands they'll burn it to the ground."

"So Elves now walk the walls of Magdan," nodded Eline, a smile playing at her lips. "However, that leaves many thousands of refugees outside city walls throughout the land. Not all will survive the winter."

"No, it's doubtful half will survive it. The Elves are doing what they can to bring them food, but we're too spread out through the realm to do a thorough job of the task."

"What of the Geni and their supporters? What fate befell them?"

"The lady sent them south. She set a few of the Borni to watch and help them survive, but no more. They won't pass the winter in comfort, if they manage to survive it."

"I'll confess it Ethor, considering her early years as a slave in that city, I'm a bit surprised at the queen's compassion for the Geni."

"Lady Ariel is the soul of compassion, Eline." That caught her attention. She noticed the grin playing at his lips.

"So, my old friend, what more do you have to tell me? You did speak of a royal command."

"I did indeed. You are commanded by the queen to take your fighters and return to Argar at the first opportunity." He laughed with delight at the bright smile that lit up her face. "It seems that Trelanth suggested to the queen that you and Lord Tanis make an efficient team, and that he would need his second at his side. Lady Ariel instantly ordered you back to Argar."

"That is glorious news indeed, old friend. I don't suppose there's any way you could magic up a sudden thaw, could you?"

"Afraid not," he laughed, "but we'll consult with Kekka about how soon we can get you back to the low lands. Now, what shall we do with the Bornani we brought here?"

"They've been training and are doing better than I expected. I'll take my hundred and return to Tanis, you keep the Bornani here with you. You'll need them when you escort Kekka on her mission to recruit more Coti tribes into our alliance."

At that point they noticed Kekka approaching. She and the Coti had been out foraging. Ethor called her over and explained what they wanted. "Eleene want go now?"

"Now? Kekka, is that possible?"

The Coti woman nodded. "Can go. Not come back. Snows too deep. Sky clear, Kekka show. Climb, go through cave, slide down mountain, reach trees. No way back."

Two days later the sky was bright and clear. Eline led her hundred warriors plus another twenty to escort Kekka safely back to the way station. She led them up into the mountains. For two days they climbed steadily upwards through the deep snows. On the third day the ground leveled off as they entered a narrow canyon.

A short way into the canyon Kekka stopped and began digging at the snow. She soon uncovered a small cave mouth. She wriggled inside and called for the others to follow. As Eline came through she found Kekka lighting torches. The cave was a lot bigger inside and she could easily stand upright. For the rest of the day the Elves went two abreast as they traveled through that cavern, it gently sloping downward.

The world was in darkness when they reached the end of the tunnel, so they rested until light returned to the world. When the sun was high, Kekka spoke to Eline. "Look there. See land level off? There you must go. Go that way, too many rocks hide in snow. Hurt, die. There where land go level. Good landing. Jump now."

Eline took a hard look at the distance of fall and swallowed hard. "Jump?"

"Yes. Jump there. Aim for tall tree. Jump." Still Eline hesitated. "Many Coti jump. Like jump. Fun."

Eline looked at Kekka who was grinning at her. "All right, I'll jump, but if I break my neck somebody shoot her for me." With that she leaped into space with the sounds of the Coti's laughter behind her. She felt as though she fell endlessly before hitting the snow in a puff and cloud of powder. With a wild shriek of laughter she surfaced and danced away toward the trees once she stopped sliding.

One by one the warriors followed, landing in the snow to roll out of the way of the next falling body. Once they were all on the ground Eline turned to wave at Kekka and Ethor who stood at the cave mouth high above. The Coti had been right, there was no way to return by that route.

As Ethor waved back, Eline turned and led her troops into the forest. Two days later they were back in Fugitive. The next day they set out for Argar. Their first stop would be at the gates of Shotar.

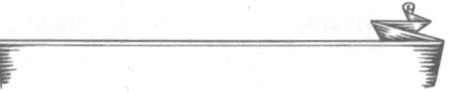

Battle at the Gates

"Lora, what troubles you?"

"Bralin, can you see the gates clearly?"

"No, there's a mist over the land."

"Is there? The sky above is clear as any I've ever seen, there's warmth in the rays of the sun, and I mistrust this."

"You think magic is afoot?"

"Don't you? It's a beautiful day, but I can't see clearly, I'm well rested and fed, yet I'm sluggish, irritable, as though after a long trek."

"Curse them, you're right. The mages are attacking us, something is about to happen."

"And I'll wager there will soon be open gates and men at arms to deal with. Spread the word, recite the counter spells, ready your bows, they're coming out. Pull everybody back into the trees and make ready."

He trotted away, softly reciting a counter spell. As silent as a forest night the Elves retreated deeper into the trees.

Inside the city the men at arms readied their weapons. This was it; the food was running out. They had twenty warriors guarding every hunter. The mages were to be hard at work, masking their movements, blinding the Elves to the danger at hand. As the massive gates began to swing open they urged their horses forward.

The royal mage paced about impatiently. He'd come up with this idea of a sortie to mask his actual activities. Every lesser mage and apprentice was focused on the task of confusing the Elves beyond the city walls. Ten hunters, each with a guard of twenty warriors, were ready at the gates. Meanwhile, the royal mage and his assistant withdrew to his inner office then stepped through a portal, never to be seen in Shotar again.

Outside, as the gates opened something unexpected happened. The surviving refugees, hoping for a delivery of food, rushed the mounted men. With nothing to offer except swords and mace blows the men at arms tried to force them back.

In a desperate rage, the refugees swarmed the first few men to exit the gates. A half dozen men were dragged down to their doom and three horses were killed before the refugees were driven off. Once the rabble had scattered in fear, the men at arms led their hunters along the trails used by the Elves as they came to bring food to the starving.

Lora was cursing as she ran. "They're using our own trails against us. Spread out, you know what to do."

The Elves vanished from the trails, yet could be seen from time to time, enough to keep the pursuit coming. Lora was the main bait, showing herself often, loosing an arrow, then darting away. She led them well off the trails, out into deeper snows. The plan had been to spread out to hunt, but the sight of all the running Elves was enough to keep the mounted troops together.

The men at arms suddenly stopped, their mounts' sides heaving, breath rising in great clouds into the winter air. The Elves had vanished. Worse yet, they could see the open fields through the trees. They'd been led back out of the forest. Swearing like a madman, the leader ordered them to split up and begin the hunt. They were there to hunt for food, not for Elves.

As the groups split up, each one was followed by the warriors of the forest. Lora cursed them again as she hadn't enough fighters to send more than eight or ten after each group. She alone followed the leader's hunting group. As the day wore on she began to grin with delight. Twenty mounted men at arms make enough noise to keep any and all game well out of sight.

The leader and his hunter were arguing heatedly as they set up camp that night, each blaming the other for the day's failure. Three guards were posted, and the rest settled down in a cold hungry camp. Dawn came and the three guards were found dead, stripped of their weapons, cloaks, and boots. The horses were gone as well.

The leader was bawling orders when the arrow pierced his chest. He sank slowly to the ground as his men formed a defensive wall, their backs to the fire. Long did they wait in the cold, but nothing else happened. No bird sang, no squirrel chattered, only the cold unloving breath of a winter wind sighing through the trees could be heard.

The men waited through the day, but nothing more happened until one man stepped away to relieve himself. He did not return. As darkness fell, three more guards were posted. Next morning they were found dead, as was the hunter, still under his cloak, a dagger buried in his heart.

The remaining men set out slowly, heading for the open fields and the safety of the gates of Shotar. That night they didn't stop, but continued on until they reached the edge of the forest. They stopped to rest and a man fell with an arrow through the back. The rest fled out into the open where an enemy would have to show themselves to get at them.

Dawn found them still awake. The new leader told them to sleep while he watched. They were in the open now, only one man on watch was needed. He sighed and silently cursed the Elves as well as the Geni as he watched. They were barely a dozen strong now, the hunter dead, and not one scrap of meat to show for it. He hoped the other units had fared better.

They hadn't. By the end of the day they were all back in the open fields, barely half the numbers that had entered the forest. Only one hunter was still alive, and he was wounded. They gathered together for protection, setting out guards and making plans to return to the gates as soon as the sun returned.

Back in the trees, Lora sighed with relief as she sensed the withdrawal of the mages's spells. Even a mage needs to sleep sometime. Her small force had managed to drive the men at arms out of the forest, but they were too few to fight them in the open. Worse yet, many of them managed to keep their horses, so the Elves dare not go out into the open fields to fight them.

Lora was still muttering when Bralin found her. "Lora, they're here."

"Who's here?"

"I know not how this came to pass, but Eline's here with a hundred warriors. Come." Grinning with delight, Lora followed him back into the trees. They soon reached Eline's camp.

"Lora, report," smiled Eline as she tossed the tired warrior some meat. Lora brought her up to speed while she ate. Eline sat listening as the girl ate her fill. "So, they're all bunched up in the open now?"

Lora nodded. "I hadn't enough people to attack them openly, Eline. We've gotten too spread out. Kern took some with him, and I left others with the families of those men out there in the fields."

"I wonder," mused Eline, "how many of those men would now renounce their allegiance to the Geni and return to their families."

"You'd offer them the chance? Many are sell swords, as easily swayed one way or the other at the drop of a gold coin."

Eline nodded her agreement. "Sadly, you have the right of it, Lora. The queen wants human allies, and we've sworn to help her find them. However, those men aren't likely allies, for they didn't come out to defend their families as your friend Garret did.

"No, these are the enemies of the queen. Rest your people, they've done their work this day. We'll deal with those who entered the queen's forests with ill intent." With that she rose, made a signal with her arm, and led her warriors out into the darkness of the nighttime forest.

Out on the open field the men on watch thought they saw movement, but the moon was suddenly obscured by a cloud. When it cleared nothing moved. They held their breath as they tried desperately to pierce the gloom, to discern the secrets it held. Once again the clouds hid the light.

The moon reappeared and, shocked to the core, they saw a wave of Elves running silently across the snows. Bow strings twanged, arrows flew to their targets, and men fell. A single shout of alarm rang out over the silent fields. Men tried to rise from their slumbers only to fall back again, arrows embedded in their bodies.

Battle cries rent the air, swords clanged against swords, blades bit deep, arrows pierced flesh, and men fell. The sun rose on white fields of snow stained red with the blood of the dead. Those who'd left the safety of the walls would not return. Their cloaks, boots, and food were gathered and distributed to the refugees at the gates. Their horses were stripped of their saddles then set loose to survive as best they could.

By the fall of darkness it was done, and Eline, with her hundred warriors, was already on the road to Argar.

KRATAC, KING OF THE Geni, paced about his audience chamber. "What? What did you say? Speak up, mage, speak up?"

"Sire, the men at arms sent to guard the hunters have failed."

The Geni king was getting more agitated by the moment. "Failed, what do you mean, they failed?"

"They're all dead, Sire. The Elves defeated them all." The mage cringed away from the ire of the king.

Finally the king stopped pacing and fuming. "Where is the royal mage? Why didn't he bring me this news himself?"

The poor messenger swallowed hard before he responded. "He'd gone, Sire. Vanished. He's nowhere to be found. We've searched everywhere, by every means available to us."

Shocked, the king retreated to his throne and seemed to shrivel into it. "It's the Witch of Elanda, she must have taken him."

"Or he fled for his life while he had the chance," muttered the messenger.

"What? What was that?"

"Nothing sire."

"Advise me, mage. What are we to do now? Well, speak up man."

The poor mage drew in a long breath then sighed. "Sire, we have but a single hope. Magdan has fallen, and the Elves have defeated us here. We should tighten up our defenses and wait for the snows to leave the lands. We can survive until then with what we have, but no longer.

"Sire, we can contact the other cities, command all troops to march as soon as the snows melt. Sire, I understand that will concede the seacoast to the pirates and sea rovers, but we have no other options. If all our troops march at once, join up into a single army, they can easily clear a path to Shotar, bring us food and supplies.

"The Elves will be forced to withdraw into the forests. With the roads clear and held by our troops we can restock the storehouses, rebuild our garrison, and bring Shotar back to its former glory."

The mage began to sweat as the king sat gazing at him. The man wasn't half of what the former royal mage had been, but perhaps he was a more able tactician. Finally the king broke the silence. "I accept your plan. I now appoint you official court mage. The task is yours, make it happen." With a wave of his hand the king dismissed his new royal mage.

As the mage withdrew from the audience chamber his apprentice stepped up beside him. "I heard all of that. You know full well what'll happen if we do this. What have you done?"

"I've bought us some time, that's what I've done. We've got a couple of moon cycles yet. Time enough to devise a better plan, or to find a way to escape and leave that inbred fool to his fate." Together they hurried away to the mage's tower.

AS THE MEN OF MAGIC retreated to their tower, outside the city gates the surviving refugees were enjoying their second day of feasting on horse meat. Better yet, the Elves had brought more cloaks and boots. New shelters were being built and older ones reinforced with these new materials.

Better yet, the Elves had begun to talk to the refugees about their burned out farms. They promised that, if the refugees would ally themselves with the Elf Queen, they would be allowed to return to their homes and rebuild. They even offered to help wherever possible.

The winter was nearing an end, and those who'd managed to survive were beginning to find a glimmer of hope. With luck another moon cycle would bring warm winds from the south.

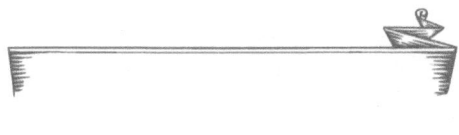

Reunion

T anis sat at his war table, slowly nursing his bowl of thin stew. He refused to take any food that the others couldn't partake of. If the people of Argar were making meals of thin stews to stretch out the food supplies, then that's what he'd eat.

"You must truly enjoy that stew," grinned Kern as he and Dera entered the warmth of the inn. "I've seen you eat little else for days."

Grinning, Tanis looked up as they approached and sat with him. "Well, truth be told, Kern, I have a great fondness for Maggie's stew, especially since the alternative is to slip into the trees for a meal of beetles and grubs. What say you, Trelanth?"

The smiling woman who approached winked at Dera. "Grubs and beetles? My Lord Tanis, Kern is the master horseman, surely he's been enjoying oats and hay with his friends in the barns."

"Ha ha ha, Trelanth. I promise the next horse you ride will be lively enough for you."

With a chuckle and a friendly pat on Kern's shoulder, Trelanth sat to table with them and thanked the smiling woman who brought her a steaming bowl. "My Lord Tanis, I bring news."

"Trelanth?"

"Before the sun sets this day we will have another hundred warriors at hand."

Tanis sat up straighter, his eyes showing his excitement. "Eline? She's escaped the mountains?"

"The same," grinned Trelanth. "How she managed this miracle I know not."

"Kern, I'll need a horse," said Tanis, his voice betraying his excitement.

"I'll go, my love," said Dera. "You stay by the fire and keep that leg warm." She rose with a warrior's grace and left the inn, heading for the barns. She had a tall horse saddled and waiting for Tanis when he arrived moments later. She stepped into his arms and hugged him as she passed him the reins.

"Tanis, my beloved brother, I beg you, speak to Eline of your feelings. You're tormented and I ache to see you this way."

"I can't, sweet Dera. I can't speak to her only to have her snatched away to another by the compulsion. That would tear the heart out of me."

"That could happen, yes, but it might be years from now, centuries, or perhaps never. Tanis, several of the Borni have told me, they don't all await the call of the compulsion. Those are special bonds, in that the couples have great things to accomplish together. Like the Queen and Lady Mearith who will set free all Elves, or perhaps it's to create a child who will rise high, do great things. The rest must find love on their own."

"You've been talking to Trelanth."

"I have, yes. We both want to see you happy. Tanis, even Lady Ariel, once informed of the problem, immediately ordered Eline back to Argar. And Eline, somehow she found a way to defeat the mountain snows to return to you. Go to her now, my brave warrior brother. Go claim your prize."

With a sigh and a wave of resolve, Tanis kissed her cheek then mounted and rode out.

Eline trotted along, her long legs easily devouring the miles. Behind her ran a hundred warriors, many of them Bornani, freed from slavery less than a year past, and yet, now hardened warriors. They topped a small rise to see a lone rider sitting on his horse, directly in their path. A wide grin of pure delight reached her face as she jogged down toward him.

As she neared the hooded rider Eline stopped and pointed past him with both arms. Her warriors continued on, passing by the rider and vanishing into the landscape. Slowly the horse stepped closer to her, and the rider dismounted, pushing back his cloak.

Her bright smile of delight faded as she saw the look of determination on his face. She tilted her head slightly as she gave him a quizzical raised eyebrow. With a deep breath to brace himself he stepped closer and reached out to take her shoulders in his hands, holding her gently in place.

"My Lord Tanis?"

"Hush now, Eline. Let me speak before my courage fails me. Eline, I can no longer await the pleasure of the compulsion. I ache inside for your nearness. If you cannot ..."

He got no further as she stepped closer and kissed him. Tanis pulled her tightly to him, his knees shaking with the power of the emotion that surged through him. He softly breathed her name as their lips parted and he hugged her even tighter. "Eline..."

"That took you long enough," she whispered. "I thought I'd have to get Ethor to make up a love potion to put in your ale."

"Eline?"

"Tanis, my beloved, my desire has ever been to be at your side since we first met. My love, I know that which you fear, for that fear is my own as well. However, hear me well, in all my long memory the Spirit Pull has never separated two who have sworn themselves to each other. I promise you; we will not be the first."

He released his hold on her slightly so he could gaze into her eyes. He was smiling now and she exulted to see it. "So, dear Eline, shall we return to Argar and declare before all?"

"If that is your wish, my love," she replied, meeting his bright smile with one of her own, "for it truly is my own wish to do so."

"Then so be it," he declared. She shrieked as he swept her up and tossed her into the saddle. He leaped up behind her and put his arms around her waist. She snuggled back against him as he took the reins from her hands and flipped them lightly. The horse turned and headed back toward the barn.

Back at the inn Trelanth smiled and relaxed. She nodded to Dera whose bright smile told Kern what he wanted to know. He was now back to being the horseman, he'd just lost his job as the second. Kern couldn't be happier.

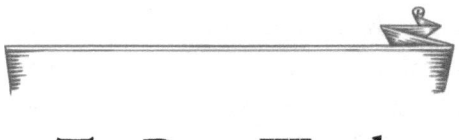

The Deep Woods

Deep in the forest Bralin sat by a warm fire, talking with Tek, Mary, Garret, and a few others. The human and Orc group had been reduced to just over a hundred souls by this time, but those who remained had managed to regain their strength. Well over half their numbers were children with a few elders, but all had become somewhat proficient with a bow.

"Well, Tek, what do you think?" asked Mary as she leaned against his shoulder. She and her daughter had gone hunting alone and had brought back a deer for the feast.

Tek grinned as he gave her a friendly nudge. "I think my work here is done. Mary, I'm so proud of you I could burst."

"The thing is," said Garret, "I agree with Tek. Everybody in the camp now can survive in the forest, most are becoming somewhat proficient with weapons as well. Now I think we should move on to the next step."

"The next step?" asked Bralin.

"Teaching these folks how to fight as a unit. Fighting an enemy one on one is one thing, fighting as a unit is another."

Ellen leaned forward and rested her elbows on her knees. "So, now you want to take us from hunter gatherers to warriors?"

"I do, sweet Ellen," he smiled as he gently caressed her cheek. "In the past moon cycle we've fought the wolf creatures twice and that other abomination once. Each time we were successful, but we've lost people each time. I think a few military tactics would increase our chances."

"Can't argue that," said Bralin. "What say you, Tek?"

"I have no knowledge or experience with military tactics. I have, however, seen the Borni work as a single unit with great success. I'm game to learn whatever you can teach. Mary?"

"I like the idea, Tek. If you say go then we go." The others gave her a strange look, and Tek was gazing into her eyes, lost from the rest of the world.

Ellen grinned and nudged Tek, breaking him from the trance. "Tek, my friend, I suggest you take Mary back to your fire and have a long talk with her. You're both becoming quite useless as things stand now."

Startled, he gazed at her, wide eyed. "What?"

"It's become quite clear to me that you two are besotted with each other. You hunt together, you gather together, you stand the watch side by side, and you get lost in each others eyes constantly. The woman has you bewitched to the point where you can no longer function. Take her back, tell her of your feelings, swear the bond with her then come back ready to go to work."

The others were somewhat startled, Tek and Mary were both blushing, and Mary was grinning with delight. "Well, deny it if you can."

Tek's mouth worked for a moment, but he made no sound. Finally he lowered his head to his hands and spoke softly. "I can't deny it. I was her slave once, and then I was set free, but now I'm enslaved again."

Mary reached out to grip his arm tightly. "Tek?"

He didn't look up. "Mary, I ..."

"Tek, you forgave me the early years, kept me and mine alive, taught us how to be strong, and then you befriended me as I had no right to expect, although I did want that. Tek, hear my words. You have shown love for me in ways no other ever did. If you truly want to swear the bond with me, I'm more than willing."

"Mary?" He looked up to meet her smiling eyes at last.

"It's my heart's desire too." She was smiling at him now and once again he was lost in her eyes.

Bralin gave him a light punch on the shoulder. "Go on man. When the gods offer treasure, for pity sake, seize it up."

He gave Tek a gentle push toward Mary who melted against him. "Well, Tek, will you bond with me?"

"Mary, I ... yes. By all the gods of mercy, yes."

"Sworn and witnessed," grinned Garret. "Now can we get back to work?"

Ellen laughed and slapped his arm. "Not on your life, sir man at arms. This is a time to celebrate."

There was laughter and dancing well into the night. As things began to settle down Tek took Mary back to their camp and snuggled her close under his cloak. "Well it's about time," giggled the eldest daughter.

"Hush you," grinned Tek as he shook a finger at the two giggling girls. Mary gently pulled his face down to hers and kissed him.

It was just at dawn when they heard the crashing in the trees and the alarm sounded. The two women who'd been on watch came racing back into the camp. "Spears and swords to the front," bawled Garret, "bows behind, quickly now."

The thing that staggered from the trees was three times as tall as a man, yet it somehow looked like a man. Giant! The Borni swept in front of the others, they had fought these things before. Bralin held up his hand as the huge monster rubbed at its eyes. "Ho, Giant, can you speak?"

Puzzled, the creature looked down at him. "What?"

Many of those they'd fought before could not, but some of the leaders could. "I asked if you can speak."

The giant nodded. "Hungry. Got food?"

Puzzled, Bralin motioned behind him. Tek soon appeared with a huge slab of meat which he offered to the giant. The huge creature was surprisingly gentle as he took the offering. "Thank. Cold." He gestured toward the fire.

Bralin nodded then stepped aside allowing the creature to approach. He was surprised at how careful it was when it sat, making sure to not hurt or frighten anyone. Suddenly Ellen approached with a water skin. "Water." She offered the prize and the giant took it gently then drained it in a single gulp.

"Thank." It chewed thoughtfully on the meat for a while then spoke again. "Where others?"

"Others?" asked Bralin.

"Like me. Others like me. Geni force me to lead others to strange lands, Geni make kill small people there. Bad thing to do. Hate Geni. No Geni here?"

"No," replied Bralin. "No Geni here. Geni enemy."

The giant nodded sagely. "Yes. Geni enemy. Geni make magic, fog mind. Force people to kill. Not want kill. Geni give no choice. See Geni now, crush like rabbit." He flexed his massive hand into a fist then relaxed it. "Who you folk?"

Bralin gestured the others back. "We're enemies of the Geni. We're forest folk. We serve the Elf Queen."

The giant chuckled and nodded. "Ah, Elf Queen. Great magic. Make Geni run like small mouse. Elf queen stop Geni fog mind, set free. Geni send demon to kill."

Bralin sighed. This creature was as much a victim of the Geni as any other. He patted his chest. "Bralin." He pointed to Tek. "Tek." Then he pointed to the giant. "You?"

The giant nodded that he understood. He was becoming much more aware now that he'd had food and water. "Brak. Brak was leader of tall folk. Geni come, fog mind, make tall folk kill small people. Small folk mighty fighters, hard to kill. Demons come, go crazy. World break, swallow demons. Brak sleep. Wake now, hungry, thirsty."

Bralin nodded. "Someone bring him more food and water. Brak, that fight was long time ago. Long gone. Geni not so strong with magic anymore. Small folk fight against the Geni. When the queen comes, we can talk to her. She may be able to help you get home."

"Brak home gone. Geni destroy. Bralin see more Brak folk?"

"No, but we might encounter some now that you're awakening."

"Awakening?"

"Long ago, when the world swallowed the demons, the Geni put all their warriors to sleep. Now they're waking them up. Perhaps we will encounter more of your people. Where should we tell them to look for you? Where will you go?"

The poor giant looked sad as he absorbed that information. Finally he sighed and looked up. "Nowhere to go, no home, no people. Brak lay down now. You good folk. Kill Brak quick, no suffer."

Suddenly Mary was beside him. Even sitting down he was still slightly taller than she was. She smiled and patted his arm. "No kill Brak. Brak stay with us, maybe find more Brak's people one day."

"Small folk let Brak stay? No kill?"

"Bralin?"

"All right, Mary. I agree with you on this. Stay with us, Brak, no kill."

The giant grinned broadly. "You good hearted folk. Brak like you. What Brak do to help?"

That was all it took. Ellen soon had the giant helping to gather firewood. When he understood about the other creatures he made himself a club and set himself to watch and defend the camp. Two days later a group of wolflike creatures attacked, but Brak slapped them down with ease.

"Brak remember nasty creatures. Geni make. Bad. Brak kill nasty creatures, Geni angry with Brak."

"Well I'm not angry with you at all, Brak," said Ellen. "You did a good job and I'm right proud of you." The giant beamed his pleasure at her praise.

Oddly enough, instead of being frightened by Brak, the giant soon became a favorite of the younger children. They shrieked with laughter as he held them up high to gather the dead branches for firewood. Two of the smaller ones often rode in his pockets as he searched out the deadfalls and pulled them from the snow, breaking up the branches for more firewood.

The hunters loved him too. Not only did he entertain the children while they hunted, but the noise he made walking through the forest and dragging back dead trees, often sent game running their way. Instead of being a drain on their resources, Brak soon became the reason for prosperity.

One day, as he was out gathering wood, he met a new band of Elves. They faced him with drawn bows, but the sight of small children peeking out of his pockets and clinging to his shoulders stayed their hands. Brak squared himself and hefted his club. "Brak no let you hurt small ones."

One of the Elves strode toward him, her arms spread wide to show she held no weapon. "I greet you, Brak, defender of small humans. My name is Ariel. We mean you and your charges no harm."

"No harm small ones?"

"We will not. I swear it."

The giant nodded and lowered his club. "You friend of Bralin?"

"We are. Can you tell us where to find our kinfolk?"

"You come. Follow Brak." With that he turned and trudged through the snow, dragging a dead tree behind him.

As Brak entered the camp he called out for Bralin. It was Tek who answered. "Bralin is out hunting, Brak. What ... My queen!" Tek dropped to one knee and, slowly, as they began to realize who this was, so did the rest of the camp. Even Brak lowered himself to one knee, allowing the children to scramble to the ground.

"Rise, my friends," smiled Ariel. "Rise and greet me with tales of your adventures. I regret it has taken so long for me to visit you."

Runners were sent to fetch the hunters and a feast was begun. The Queen of the Elves had come. She was in the camp. The fires were built up and food soon in the cooking pots, meat roasting on the spits, and the music of drum and flute filling the air.

The people gathered to meet the queen and her personal guard stood the watch for the camp. "Bralin, you folk have managed miracles," said Ariel.

"Nay, Lady Ariel, it is the folk themselves who have performed the miracles. We Elves now have little to do except sleep and eat what the camp hunters bring to cook for us." There was a great round of laughter at that.

"So tell me, my new allies, how came you to be here? Are you the families of those men at arms who remain behind the walls of Shotar?"

"Most of us, Lady Ariel, yes," replied Ellen.

"But not you," said Mearith. "I've heard of a woman who brought her man at arms out of Shotar with her, and allied herself with the Elves, placing her warrior at their service. Might you be this woman?"

"I am that woman, Lady, and this man is my loyal warrior. We are bound by the terms of our agreement. Have you a task for Garret?"

"No," smiled Mearith, "for I can see his skills have been put to good use here and so it should remain. Ariel, my delight, what think you of our new allies?"

"I'm impressed and thrilled with these good folk. Tell me, good people, when the snows leave the lands, will you return to the farms to rebuild?"

"We've been discussing this, Lady," said Ellen. "We believe we have a different plan that might work, if the Elves will agree to it."

"Oh? Please, share your thoughts with us. What do you have in mind?"

"Lady, the farms were all too easily defeated by the Reavers," said Mary. "Also, we were ever plagued by bands of brigands. As well, we suspect the war against the Geni may not be ended easily. It would bear no worth to rebuild farms that marching soldiers could easily capture and destroy.

"With that in mind, we thought we might be permitted to live as the ancient Elves did, in a forest village, built right here in this place. We can build walls to protect us, and the cliffs will do so as well. We aren't so far from the open fields that we couldn't plant crops there, but return to the safety of the village at darkness or danger."

"If this is truly your desire, good people, then permission is granted," replied Ariel. "However, I must warn you, there is no true safety behind walls. My own people learned this to their lasting dismay, and you have recently learned the same in Shotar.

"Be certain to leave yourselves a passage into the forest, should the force sent against you be too strong. In the trees you can run free, confound those who pursue you, and elude all capture until you find your allies."

"That's good advice and we'll heed it," said Garret.

"I'll keep a small detail of Elves near you always, in case they're needed and to bring message to me and from me back to you."

"Lady Ariel," said Tek, "with your permission, I should like to remain with these folk, perhaps as part of that detail."

Ariel leaned toward him and poked him lightly on the shoulder. "You have a story to tell, sir. Every sense I have tells me you have a special reason for this request."

"Alas, you have guessed the right of it, my queen," he sighed. "When I was a slave I served this woman's family. Although a demanding mistress, she none the less refused to allow the use of the whip or torture."

"Yes, and what was my reward for my kindness?" grinned Mary, winking at Ariel. "I was abused and bullied by this ungrateful beast when I was at my most vulnerable, cast out, hungry and forsaken."

"Tek, is this true?"

"Sadly, it's true, my queen. I took the opportunity to extract vengeance, but, now she has enslaved me once again."

Ariel's eyes darkened at that, but then she saw the grin of mischief on his face. "Enslaved?" exclaimed Mary, a twinkle in her eye. "I hunt and gather your food, cook for you, mend your clothes, and then warm your bed at night. How does this make you the slave?"

"It does because I have become so spoiled with your cooking I am now bound to you forever, for I'd surely starve elsewise."

"My cooking, that's what holds you to me?"

"Yes, well, that and other delights," he grinned as he pulled her closer, reveling in her sweet laughter.

"Tek, behave, you beast, the queen is here for pity sake," laughed Mary as she poked him in the ribs then kissed his cheek fondly.

Ariel smiled and relaxed. "So, have you two truly bonded?"

"We have, Lady," replied Tek. "None were more surprised than the two of us."

"I'm amazed and yet truly happy for you both," said Ariel. "Yes, Tek, you may remain with your lady companion. Now, explain to me how you came to adopt a giant."

Ellen told the tale of Brak wandering into their camp, still half asleep and confused. She told of how he wanted only to find a place of peace well away from the Geni. When the tale was told Ariel called Brak to her. He came and sat a respectful distance away.

Ariel smiled at him then spoke. "Brak, can you tell me what the Geni did to you? How did they make you fight my people?"

"Geni make head hurt, Elf Queen. Head hurt, mind foggy. Voice in head say kill Elf, pain go away. Voice lied. Always more pain, more Elf to kill. Brak hate Geni. Hope Geni no find with Ellen people."

Ariel thought for a moment. "Brak, that stone you wear around your neck, what is that?"

"Is gift from small one. Ellen child. Girl child make, gift for Brak."

"May I touch it?"

He nodded then took it off and passed it to her. Ariel held it in her cupped hands and closed her eyes. The stone began to glow with a brilliant light. She held it so for a few moments then the light subsided.

Smiling, Ariel passed it back to him. "Wear it always, Brak. No Geni can touch your mind as long as you wear that stone. You are free of them now."

He held the stone in his huge hands, gazing at it with a wistful smile. Finally he put it back around his neck. "Thank, Great Elf Queen. Brak wish he make friend with Elf Queen long ago. When Elf Queen go to fight Geni, call Brak. Brak help."

"I will surely call on you, my new friend," smiled Ariel. "For now, I need you to remain here to help Ellen and her people."

He smiled and nodded, patting the now shiny stone that lay against his huge chest. "Brak stay. Help friends."

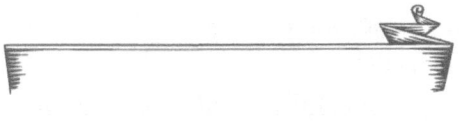

A Change of Plans

High in the mage tower in Shotar the new royal mage stared at the now quiet seeing stone. He wasn't sure what had just happened, but he was pleased that it had. He could now take good news to the king. While he hurried away to the hall of audience, a cloaked and frightened woman slipped quietly out of a city far to the east, taking her bonded companion with her.

The shivering woman huddled deeper into her thin cloak as she grasped her companion's hand tightly and hurried him along. The basket he carried was heavy and slowing him down, but he made no complaint. As the night slowly faded to dawn they fought their way past the refugees towards the forested hills beyond.

The sun was already up when they reached the trees. A few paces further and their way was blocked by three Elves with drawn bows. It was the Elves who got the real surprise as the woman spoke. "Oh thanks be to the gods, we found you. Quickly now, take me to your queen."

The lead Elf just grinned as he lowered his bow and stepped toward her companion. To his great surprise, the man reached up to remove his own slave collar and tossed it away. "It seems I won't be needing this anymore."

"I hated keeping that on you, my love," she said as he leaned over and kissed her cheek.

The Elf warrior looked the two strangers over for a moment then spoke. "I see that you two have a tale to tell, and I do want to hear it.

Come, we'll sit beside a warm fire and eat our fill, and then you can tell me your story."

The woman reached toward him imploringly. "Please, you must take me to your queen."

"First you speak with me and then I decide what happens next," he replied. "Reena."

"Yes, my Lord Arlon."

"Away now to the camp and prepare to move out. I have a sense we may need to go soon. Oh, wake the mage."

"Yes, my lord." The young Elf sped away and he turned back to the woman and her companion. "Come on, you two, let's get you warm and feed you." With that he turned and strode away. The two fugitives from Draton followed closely.

They soon arrived at a well established camp and Arlon started issuing orders. "Somebody bring these folks better traveling clothes and boots, warmer cloaks as well. Now for some food, sit, join me."

Arlon sank easily down beside the warm fire and they gratefully joined him. He offered them food then the Elf spoke. "Good sir, I have only a small amount of oshar, but I'll share what I have."

Arlon reached out to grip his shoulder in a friendly manner. "My friend, oshar isn't a food, it's a poison. Here, have some venison, and this stew is delightful."

The woman looked distressed. "He'll die without the oshar, won't he?"

"No girl, he'll awaken. I was young when the great shining ship brought the humans to this world, I fought at the gates of Elanda when the world was broken, and I have never tasted that poison. Oshar dulls an Elf's natural senses and shortens their life. A few days without it and our friend will begin to step lighter, talk to the forest and winds, and sing with the renewed senses that awaken."

She gazed at him for a long moment. "You speak the truth."

"I do. You're a mage?"

"I am. No, no, I do not reveal your location to those within the city, I cloak it."

"She speaks truth," said another voice.

"I've seen your face in the seeing stone many times," said the woman, "yet only when you wish it."

"You're actually quite good," she grinned as she sat beside the human mage. "A few centuries more and you'd make a fine mage. Tell me, why have you come to us?"

"I have an urgent message for the queen, that and we seek sanctuary."

"Tell me," said Arlon.

"This man is not my slave, nor has he been for a long time. He's my bonded companion. The Geni are beginning to suspect, and so we fled, seeking sanctuary among the Elves who run free."

"Fair enough," said Arlon. "You spoke of a message for the queen. What is it?"

"The mages have ways to speak across the leagues of the lands. Recently the king in Shotar has called for all men at arms to march to Shotar as soon as the snows begin to melt. Shotar is under siege as is Draton. The king orders all the cities to be abandoned and the warriors to gather at Shotar, bringing food and supplies."

"Like that'll happen," chuckled Arlon.

"Actually, it will," said her Elf companion. "The cities of Draton and Elb are ever beset by sea rovers. With the sea raiders at one hand and the Elves at the other, these cities will be impossible to defend. The overlords of Draton and Elb plan to march to the aid of Shotar then seize the throne for themselves."

"This is disturbing news," said Arlon. "How is it you know of these plans?"

The man chuckled easily. "Slaves hear much and share it freely among themselves in the kitchens and hallways of the rich and powerful. As soon as I heard about this I told Sheila immediately."

"I knew the time for us to escape had come," said the woman. "Our hope is you will take us in as exchange for the information."

"The information is welcome indeed," said Arlon, "but we'd have taken you in anyway." He turned and spoke to the mage. "Contact Trelanth at Argar. Tanis needs to know of this. Trelanth can inform the queen.

"Now then, my new friends, just how many men at arms will we be facing?"

"Nearly two thousand strong from Draton," replied the Elf, "and another three thousand from Elb. The bulk of the king's forces were always stationed at the sea to protect from the raiders. The fool couldn't conceive of an attack from within the kingdom or from the north."

Arlon thought for a moment then spoke again. "Now for the big question. How many slaves are within those walls?"

"I thought you might want to know this, so, when Brill brought me the news I made a quiet survey. There are over four thousand slaves in the city of Draton and still more within Elb. When the warriors march they'll bring most of them with the advance."

Arlon was surprised at that. "They will? Why?"

"The cities will be left to the tender mercies of the sea rovers. When the people learn of the march they'll revolt and there'll be a bloodbath. The ruling Geni will slaughter the rest then keep the slaves for themselves. They'll be on the march within a moon cycle."

"Dammit." Arlon surged to his feet. "Has Trelanth been alerted?"

"She has, my Lord Arlon."

"It's not going to be enough. Contact her again. Tell her I must speak with the queen personally, Lord Tanis as well." The mage nodded then sank into a trance. In mere moments a bright light appeared.

Arlon reached a hand toward his two new friends. "Come, the queen awaits." They followed closely as he stepped through the portal.

They landed in the great room of an inn. Arlon instantly dropped to one knee before a female Elf. If Sheila had expected a woman clad in gold and finery, she was mistaken. The woman before her was dressed as a warrior, and she moved like one.

"Rise, my friends. Come, tell me why Arlon has brought you to me with such urgency."

"Lady Ariel, this woman is Sheila, a mage from the city of Draton. This man is her bonded companion, Brill," said Arlon as he reached his feet.

"Sheila, this is Queen Ariel, tell her all you've told me, quickly now."

She did. Ariel sat quietly, listening attentively, trying not to miss a single detail. "Do you know which road they will take to reach Shotar?" she asked as Shiela finished her tale.

"I overheard them talking of it, Lady," said Brill, his eyes carefully averted from her face.

"Look at my eyes, Brill," said Ariel as she reached out to tip his chin up. "You are slave no longer. You and your lady companion are welcome here in Fugitive."

"Fugitive? Is that where we are?" asked Sheila. "We planned to try for it, but doubted it truly existed."

"It does and we are in that place," replied Ariel. "Now, Brill, the road?"

"They were of two minds on it, Lady. Some wanted to travel separate roads to increase their chances of success. Still others don't trust, and so all are planned to march together, first Elb, and then, when they reach and liberate Draton, all together march to Shotar."

Another man spoke for the first time. "So, Argar is to be spared," said Tanis. "That's a piece of good news. This path will take them through Kress though. What are their plans for Kress?"

"First to join with, and then betray Kress. That is the plan as far as we know."

"As far as you know?" asked Ariel.

"Lady, I can only tell you of what I knew when we left this morning past."

"You're right, my friend," sighed Ariel. "Do you know of the numbers we face?"

"Lady, there will be at least five thousand men at arms with twice as many slaves."

"What? They're bringing out the slaves?"

"Yes, Lady," said Sheila. "They plan to betray the king and take the throne for themselves. The cities left behind will be defenseless against the sea rovers. The slaves are quite valuable, and so they will be brought with the army."

"By all the gods," exclaimed Ariel. "Mearith."

"Yes, my delight, a great opportunity approaches, but it comes with great danger. What do you want to do?"

"You know full well what I want to do. Someone fetch Marc, Drakkat, Gormin, and Freida as well." She tossed a stone to Mearith then began to pace. "Call Evan for me. I'll want his advice too."

As they set about gathering her advisers, Ariel closed her eyes and called. "Trelanth."

A voice spoke softly in her mind. "I am here, my Queen."

"I need you, Kern and Dera here as soon as possible. Call them to you and I'll open a portal."

"They are beside me as we speak, Lady."

"Then come." Ariel focused her mind and a bright light appeared in the middle of the room. A moment later three people stepped through. Evanseth, and Orin arrived mere seconds later. When all had gathered, Ariel outlined all she had learned.

Orin turned to Sheila and spoke softly to her. "You are certain of your information?"

"As certain as any can be, my Lord."

"She speaks truth, my Queen," he sighed as he turned back to Ariel.

"All right, good people, my beloved and trusted advisers, give me your thoughts on this. My Lord King?"

Evanseth sighed and nodded. "This is unexpected, yet an opportunity that cannot be ignored. However, their numbers will be too great to defeat even if you weren't as strung out along the highways as you are now. Ariel, I can easily see a further complication."

"Oh?"

"As the cities empty out it is likely the refugees and the others left behind will try to follow the army as it marches inland."

"That'll be a bloody nuisance," muttered Darkkat.

"And one we will have to contend with," sighed Ariel. "Come, people. What do we do here?"

"I think it's rather nice of them to bring the slaves out for us," grinned Tanis. "I also think it's good of them to take the back road to Shotar leaving Argar well out of the action."

"Indeed," said Ariel, "so how do we defeat them, Tanis?"

He thought for a moment then grinned. "Arlon, what think you? Me, Kern, and the Reavers, mounted on our swift ponies, savage their flanks then ride into the forest. You and your troops await them there. We don't have the number to fight them openly, but if the Reavers can lure them into the trees, a few at a time ..."

"I like it," agreed Arlon. "So, you and your savages pull some of them into the forest on both sides of the road where our troops are waiting to thin them out even more. If we do this right, all the attention will be on us at the front of the army. That's when another group can strike at the back, perhaps freeing many of the slaves. I believe that's the group you should lead, my queen."

"Oh? Why me in particular?"

"Lady, by now the entire land knows you are the one who frees the slaves. Every slave in that column will be secretly praying you appear to rescue them. They'll be ready to stampede toward the trees at the first sign of trouble."

"He's right, Ariel," agreed Evanseth. "However, the moment you appear the men at arms who guard the slaves plus those at the back of the column will attack you. The human camp followers probably will as well. You'll need troops of your own with you."

"I know. I'll take the royal Guard and the Orcs with me."

"That won't be enough," replied Evanseth, somewhat aghast that Ariel would face an army with so few at her side.

"It will be if I go too," said a soft voice as a powerfully built woman rose to her feet.

"My beloved sister, there is no need for you to leave the forge," smiled Ariel as she gave the woman a gentle hug then released her.

"No, Ariel, it's time for me to face them. When you leave for battle I will be at your side."

"As will I," declared an Orc woman.

"Rakka, someone needs to be here to lead the clan ..." said Drakkat.

"Saggit and Kreen can handle things here until we get back. You will lead the Scratite to war at the Queen's side and I'll stand beside my friend, the Lady Freida."

"So be it," he rumbled in that impossibly deep voice. "When do we start?"

"Easy, my savage friend," chuckled Ariel. "We're still working on that. Randall, are you here, old friend?"

"Right here, Ariel." Smiling, he stepped forward, leaning on his cane.

"Advise me. What's the first move?" She swept aside the things from the table then set down an empty bowl. "Here lies Shotar, and here is Kress, then Draton, Elb, and Magdan. What do you suggest we do?"

Randall studied the layout for a moment then spoke. "You've already taken Magdan. They must know this, that's why they chose the road through Kress. I expect they're already low on provisions, so they'll be expecting to get more there.

"I'd let them form up at Draton, wait until they're far enough out on the road so they can't get back behind walls, and then hit them. It's too early in the year for them to gather any food supplies on the road, so a good many of them will be hungry by then. Tired and hungry men make mistakes. Hit them hard and often, never let them rest."

"That's good advice," said Ariel. "Mearith? Arlon?"

"I agree, my delight. That's the time to attack them. We steal as many of their provisions as we can, set free as many slaves as possible, and do what we can to cut down their numbers before they reach Kress.

"Sheila, do you know of the plan for Kress. Will they include Kress in the group, or will they try to take it by force?"

"I'm sorry, Lady Mearith, I have no idea at all about this."

"It would be good if they'd fight among themselves, but, no matter," sighed Mearith. "Arlon?"

"I agree, this is the best plan and the right place to strike. Lady Ariel, we need to abandon our current plan and draw all our forces together."

"I know," replied Ariel, as she began pacing. "We're far too spread out right now and they probably know this. Evan, I'd like to borrow a few more of your mages. I don't want to put them in any danger, but I do want them to blind the Geni to our movements."

Evanseth nodded and Orin stepped forward. "Where do you want them, my queen?"

Ariel gestured at the table. "There. We have people in the forests and at the gates of every city. The Geni know they're there. I'd prefer they continue to think they remain there, and not see our movements."

"It shall be as you require, my Queen. I'll station one or two near each city. As the great army sets out those mages can join you. As you free new slaves they can usher them through portals to Elfhome. By the end of day they will be in place and at work." A glowing portal appeared and he stepped through.

"Now for the other problem," mused Ariel.

"Other problem, my delight?" asked Mearith.

"As the Geni empty the coastal cities the lands will be left defenseless against the sea rovers. They'll raid at first, but then they'll probably inhabit the area and we'll have another enemy to deal with."

"One thing at a time, Ariel," said Randall. "The sea rovers will be no threat to you until long after the Geni have been dealt with. They may even turn out to be possible allies. Focus on the battle at hand first."

Ariel smiled and gave his shoulder a friendly squeeze. "Straight through the heart of the matter as always, Randall. Is it any wonder I seek your counsel as often as I do? As you say, first things first.

"All right, people, back through the portals, send out your runners, gather your forces, and join Arlon at the forests of Draton. I will set out with my people on the morrow for we have the longest trek of all."

So saying, she created a glowing portal and Arlon stepped through. Tanis and Kern left next. "Evan, I fear that your task may be harder. If we free so many thousands of Bornani, you will be sorely taxed in Elfhome."

"Send them to me, my Queen. We'll be ready." With that he stepped through a portal and was gone.

"Now, Sheila," said Ariel. "There is room here in Fugitive for you and your companion. Will you stay as my loyal subjects, or will you seek your fortunes elsewhere?"

"Lady, to be accepted by you and to serve you is more than we dared to hope for. What would you have us do?"

"Your companion must learn the ways of the forest and combat, but your skills would be useful in keeping prying eyes away from this place. Can you do that? Will you?"

"I can and I will with a happy heart, my Queen."

"Then this man will help you find what you need. He is Marc, headman of Fugitive. Marc, find them a home, put them to work."

"Should I feed them up a bit first?"

"Fine idea, Marc," grinned Ariel. "Drakkat, I'd prefer to leave the Scraitie here to defend Fugitive."

"From who?" he grunted. "Shotar is crippled, and Ethor has made a pet of every pigman in the mountains. Marc, along with Gormin and his folk can easily defend Fugitive. We're going with you."

She laughed with delight at that, giving his broad shoulder a pat. "And glad I am of it, old friend. Prepare, people. We march on the morrow."

So it was. When the sun rose next day the Scraitite warriors were mounted and ready as Ariel, Mearith, and Freida, along with the Royal Guard, rode out of the gates of Fugitive. They had a long ride ahead of them, and the snow was still deep in the forest, but that didn't deter them at all.

The Road to Kress

Kern sat brooding as he stared into the fire. Dera was concerned for him and mentioned it to Tanis. He wasn't happy either. It had taken many more days to prepare for the journey than Tanis would have liked. He'd left only twenty warriors to defend Argar, but he'd had no choice. Only ten had remained to harry the gates of Shotar.

Worse yet, they'd elected to travel through the forest, cutting many leagues off the journey, but the snows lingered deep in the trees and hills. The going was hard and there was little food for the horses. That's what had Kern worried.

With a sigh of resignation, Tanis sank to the ground beside Kern and extended his hands to the warmth of the fire. "Talk to me, brother. How bad is it?"

"It's bad, Tanis. The snows are deeper than we thought in the heart of the forest. There's no food for the horses and they grow weak. They're tough, and game for anything, but if we don't get them some food and rest soon, they'll be useless for the coming war. I won't ask a starving horse to carry me in a fight or flight battle."

"I do agree, my friend, I do, but what's the alternative?"

Kern sighed. "We've been using the three big horses to carry the grain for the rest, but it's enough for only a handful for each once a day. Somehow we have to find a better way to break the trail, make it easier for them to travel. As soon as possible get out of the trees and onto the roads where the snows are nearly gone. Give them three of four easy days where they can graze as they go."

"Kern, we haven't the time for this."

"Then we'll be on foot when the action starts."

Tanis started to swear. "Dammit all anyway. We need ..." A shout interrupted his rant.

"Giant in the camp!"

"Giant?" Tanis leaped to his feet and saw the huge form making its way carefully towards him with two Elves and a human woman in tow.

"My Lord Tanis," called one Elf. "We've come to rescue you."

"Rescue me? Tek, what the hell are you talking about? While we're at it, why have you brought a giant into my camp?"

"This man is Brak, a friend," grinned Tek, "and this woman is my bonded companion, Mary."

"A pleasure," replied Tanis. "So, I ask again, why are you here? Aren't you supposed to be guarding the new forest village?"

"It's empty now," replied Tek. "We had a full meeting and decided you needed your warriors, so we took everybody who couldn't fight and dropped them off at Argar. The rest of us are here."

"The rest of you?"

"We are nearly sixty fighters strong. They're camped just at the edge of the clearing on your back trail. We came ahead because Brak wants to talk to you."

"I've heard of you, Brak the Tall," smiled Tanis as he offered his hand. It disappeared into the giant's gentle grip. "Tell me, how can I help you?"

"Lord Tanis not help Brak. Brak help Lord Tanis. Snows deep in trees, horses no food. Lord Tanis need strong horses. Brak walk first, make easy trail for horse to walk, save strength."

"By all the gods," said Kern as he rose to his feet. "That would be a blessing beyond measure."

The giant turned to him. "You Kern, horse leader. You tell horses Brak friend, no be scared. Brak not harm."

"I will indeed, my tall friend. Come." With Dera to support his bad leg, Kern led the giant to the herd of horses. They were nervous at first, but soon understood he meant no harm. The horses began to sniff at him, then mill around him, accepting him as a friend.

A look of bliss reached the giant's face as the horses rubbed against him and, very gently, he began to pet them, scratching lightly at their backs and eliciting many snorts of pleasure.

The next morning Brak set out in the direction of the road between Shotar and Kress. He kicked aside and trampled down the drifts, shook the hanging snow from the branches, and made as wide a path as he could. The traveling was a lot easier, and they made much better time.

Two days later they reached the open fields and the road. The snows were nearly gone from the fields, and the unharvested crops of grain and hay were a banquet for the horses. Tanis chafed at the delay, but he gave them three days to rest and recover.

They were in the open now and Trelanth informed Tanis that there was still plenty of time. The army was just leaving Elb. By the time it could reach Draton Tanis would be in Arlon's camp. They could go slower now, allowing the horses time to graze and grow strong again.

THE ROYAL MAGE OF SHOTAR sat back from his scrying stone and sighed. "Well I'll be damned."

"Sir?" asked his apprentice.

"It worked. That fool plan I made up actually worked. They've marched from Elb this day, men at arms, three thousand strong. I must inform the king." With that he hurried away.

King Kratac sat listening to the mage babble on. "Three thousand, you say. The entire garrison?"

"Yes, Sire, and they'll join up with the men of Draton and Kress. Sire, the siege of Shotar will be lifted."

"That is good news indeed, mage. I should have had the other one beheaded and promoted you long ago. Yes, the sea rovers will take those two cities, but once we have the Elves defeated, we can regain them easily enough. Well done, mage, well done."

The mage withdrew from the audience chamber and returned to his tower, calling his apprentice to him. "Quietly now. The king is busy plotting and planning. Now is our chance."

"Sir?"

"Don't be a fool. When was the last time you could see the Elves in the forest clearly? No, the forest is full of mages of the High Born, and they're led by the mad Witch of Elanda returned. We're no match for them and neither is that pitiful army. Think about it, hordes of demons were unable to defeat them, what are our chances?"

"Sir, what will we do?"

"Quietly seek out the south lands. It's hot as hell there, and half barren, but the old mage towers should still be standing, perhaps even with an intact library. Find me an empty one and we'll go there, learn what we can. I seek power, not the petty rule of unruly lands, but true power. Find us a tower with a library, my friend, then we'll abandon these fools to their fate."

The apprentice nodded then set to work.

While the young student searched and the mage studied up on portal spells, the Elves marched. Small band by small band they rejoined with their leaders on the road to Kress and the forests beyond. They came down from the mountains, out of the forests, away from the small villages they protected, and like springs of water that slowly run together to make streams and then gather to make rivers, they moved silently towards the oncoming army.

Each night, as they stopped to rest, Ariel looked into the distance, seeking them out, noting their progress, and then turned her attention to the army of the Geni. She realized she'd have to pick up her pace if she wanted to reach Arlon before he engaged the enemy. As she cast her gaze over the army her heart ached for the thousands of Elves she saw there, shivering in the cold.

"Have patience a little longer, my brothers and sisters," she said softly. "Just a little longer, I'm coming."

Ariel rose and joined Mearith and her guard. She noticed Olan sitting slightly apart, staring into the fire. She sat beside him. He started to rise, but she patted his shoulder to settle him back. "Relax, old friend. Tell me what troubles you."

He sighed deeply and gazed into the fire for a long moment before he spoke. "Lady, you should relieve me of my post in your guard."

"Why would I want to do that?" They others had fallen silent to listen.

"Because I'm weak, my Queen," he replied.

"Weak?"

"Yes. Lady, in Magdan Korath stood face to face with his old master and stayed his hand. Sadly, I had not the strength to do the same. I slew him even though he was unarmed and helpless."

"Tell me of it, old friend. Tell me of the rage and that which drove it so fiercely."

Again he sighed and gazed into the flames. "I was young, yet driven by the needs of the young to mate with another slave in our household. We were lucky, Master was an Orc and a practical man. He didn't care who mated with who as long as the females provided him with new and strong slaves. We were quite happy, my Ella and little Peg.

"One day a new Geni came to rule over Kress. As soon as he saw me smiling at Ella he put a sword through her heart then cut Peg's throat while I was being whipped. He threw Master a gold coin then had me thrown out of the gates to die in the cold. I survived.

"I endured the awakening, or the madness, as I thought it to be, and managed to survive in the forest for a few years until I was stumbled upon by Lady Mearith who took me to Fugitive where I met you.

When I saw that same Geni the rage welled up inside me and I lost control. My only thought was to kill him.

"I thought that would finally take the pain from my soul, but it burns there still. Even now I am compelled to hurry southwards to meet the oncoming enemy. Lady, my mad desires will surely cause me to betray us at some point."

Mearith spoke up then, a bright smile on her face. "Olan, tell me of this ache inside you, this mad desire to find the oncoming enemy."

The old fellow was puzzled by her smile and light teasing tone. "Lady Mearith?"

"You used an interesting word to describe this feeling of yours, Olan. You said a mad desire compels you to go south, to seek out the oncoming enemy."

"I believe I expressed it clearly, Lady. That's how it feels."

Suddenly the light of understanding reached Ariel's eyes. "Think now, Olan, dear friend, think clearly. Is this a strong desire to kill, or is it merely a powerful desire to find the enemy army?"

Puzzled, he thought for a moment. "No, Lady, I have no thoughts of killing, just the need to find the enemy. What other reason could there be to find an enemy except to kill him?"

Ariel smiled with pure delight as she gently squeezed his shoulder. "Olan, my fine guardsman, think now. Let your thoughts rest, not on the marching men at arms, but on the thousands of slaves who are accompanying them. Might there not be one among them who is equally driven to hurry towards us?"

Mearith's grin widened as the light of understanding began to reach his eyes. "You mean?"

"Yes, my friend," said Mearith, "I believe you're in the grip of the Spirit Pull, or the compulsion as you call it. Rest easy, warrior, your reward draws nearer each day we march toward them. I have the beginnings of an idea how we can satisfy your need and help free the slaves at the same time."

Ariel turned to Mearith. "Talk to me, my heart. What madness are you planning now?"

"When we find the enemy, Olan and I will slip into the slave corrals. We will go unnoticed in the crush of so many. Once there Olan can claim his prize and we can position ourselves near the guards. When you attack the army all eyes will track to that action. Olan and I will slay the guards and start the slaves moving towards the forest. That's when the rest of the troops can come to our aid. If we do this right we can get them all out with relative ease."

"My heart, the instant you act the guards, as well as the camp followers will all attack you."

"The Townsfolk? The former slave owners? They run in terror of the wild Elves of the forest. This will work, Ariel, my delight. Give me a dozen fighters and a mage then attack the front. We'll have the elves into the trees before the men at arms understand what's happening."

"Mearith, you're certain of this plan?"

"I am, my treasure. I've been working on it for a while now. I need one other with me so Olan can claim his prize and we'll be ready."

Freida moved closer and sat with them. "I'll be one of those you need, Lady Mearith. I will accompany you and Olan into the corrals."

Ariel reached out to grip her shoulder. "Sister?"

"This was ever the promise we both made so long ago, my Queen. It's time for me to do my part. You get their attention then Lady Mearith and I will set them free and stand against those who would prevent their escape."

"And I'll stand right at your side, my friend," said Rakka as she stood and moved closer.

Suddenly a wolfish grin reached Ariel's face. "Yes, and so will the Scratite. Yes, Mearith, my heart. You three enter the pens. Once I have the army's attention, you set them free and start them moving towards the forest. The Orcs will defend their retreat while the Royal Guard escorts them to the mages and the portals to Elfhome."

"My queen, you shouldn't ride to battle against so many without a personal guard," said Korath.

Ariel reached out to grip his shoulder lightly. "Korath, my ever practical friend, Arlon will have a thousand in the forest on one side of the road and Tanis will have another thousand on the opposite side. I'll take Kern and the Reavers as my personal guard. Will that satisfy?"

He grinned sheepishly. "Yes, my queen. The Reavers are a bunch of wild savages. You'll be safe enough with them."

"It's decided then," said Ariel. "We have a plan. Be at peace, Olan, in less than a cycle of the moon you will have your prize and your reward."

Slow March

It had only been three days since they'd left the gates of Elb. Sayta sighed as she plodded along beside the horse drawn litter that carried her aged master. They'd been faced with a hard choice, leave Elb and follow the army, or remain to be killed by the sea rovers. Her master had known the Geni would take Sayta from him if he chose to stay. He only hoped he would survive the journey to Shotar.

The first big surprise they got was when they emerged from the city gates. The hundreds of refugees were there, and the men at arms drove them back, but the Elves didn't attack. They all wondered about that, especially the soldiers. Where were those Elves?

Many days passed and the snow continued to melt. Unfortunately it made travel no easier, especially for those who weren't near the vanguard. The remaining snow had been a pleasure compared to the mud they now faced. The horse slipped and struggled and so did she.

Sayta wasn't young anymore, and the hard life she'd led had left her weakened. Worse, they hadn't been able to bring a lot with them. They had to ration what little food they had. She was down to one bowl of oshar per day by the time they neared Draton.

Let the old fool die," growled an Orc who plodded along beside them. "I'll take you on, ride the horse, and you can walk more easily beside me, holding to the stirrup. We'll sell the wagon to another for more food."

Sayta blushed and looked away to mop the brow of her aged master. In truth, the Orc's proposal was tempting, for she bore no love for the cruel man she tended. She nodded noncommittally and continued on. However she did take the Orc's advice and clung to the horse's harness, making the walking somewhat easier.

Nearly a moon cycle had passed by the time they reached Drayton, but there she managed to gain some rest. The men of Draton were already outside the gates and waiting when they arrived. It took several days to sort out the mass of humans, Orcs, a few Dwarves, and a small number of Geni.

While they fought and argued over the marching order, Satya managed some rest, but something new was happening. A sudden ache arose inside her, a burning desire to begin the journey. She ached with the desire to break free and race toward Kress. She didn't understand it, but it terrified her.

On the day they were to begin the march it was discovered that her master had died in the night. A fight over his belongings ensued which brought the guards, the former city watch. They quickly broke up the fight, confiscated the old man's money and few possessions, then escorted Satya into the massive group of slaves held in a loose corral. She'd either be auctioned off in Shotar or killed as useless if she failed on the journey.

She sat in the trampled muck and shared the last of her oshar with a child who'd lost his parents in the press of people. The huge army and its thousands of slaves set out for Kress. The Geni overlords rode in the vanguard with a large personal guard. Behind them rode the mounted men at arms, next marched the foot soldiers, followed by the slaves who tended the horses, plus the wagon loads of food and camp supplies.

Next came the slaves who marched under guard, nearly eight thousand of them. They were in the middle of the slowly moving mass and heavily guarded. They were the wealth of the Geni masters and had to be protected from marauding wild Elves.

Behind them came the wealthy of the two cities with the few personal slaves they'd been allowed to keep. At the last marched the tradesmen, merchants, poor and then refugees. In all the entire thing was over a league long.

Arlon stood within the forest, watching as the huge mass slowly began to move away from the city walls. Mexah stood beside him, grinning. "From here I see more Elves than I've seen in one place since the day we fled Elanda."

Arlon grunted his agreement. "The queen will be thrilled. However, we're outnumbered by nearly six to one with fighters. It won't be easy to get them out."

"There is that," said Mexah. "Ah, the mage comes with news."

A woman in mages robes hurried toward them. "All is in readiness, my Lord Arlon," she said as she arrived. "Four mages who are gifted with portals are even now pacing the slaves as they march. They'll be nearby and ready to move them to Elfhome whenever the time comes. Others are masking our movements and those of our kin."

"Excellent," replied Arlon. "Is there any news of the queen?"

"The queen has joined with Lord Tanis and they approach as we speak. They'll arrive on the morrow. The Queen sends word she has a plan to free the slaves."

"That is good news indeed. So, by the grin on your face I can see there's more."

"The Lady Freida rides with her."

"The Princess has left the forge?"

"She has, and rides beside the queen, the Scratite Orcs ride as her personal guard. She comes to free the slaves and to avenge herself on her former masters."

Arlon sighed and turned his gaze back to the masses of people in the fields below. "By all the gods, Mexah, outnumbered six to one or not, the odds have just shifted in our favor."

While Arlon watched from the forest ridge, Sayta burned with desire to begin, but the process was slow. The day was well along when the slaves began their slow march under guard. By nightfall they could still see the walls of Draton. By the coming of the dawn her mad desire had changed, she now burned to race away into the forest.

Satya walked slowly, careful not to fall. The mud was treacherous, and to fall would mean being trampled to death. By the end of day she was staggering from hunger and fatigue. On the bright side, the camp cooks also had to feed the slaves. It was only a bowl of oshar, but it was food and it renewed her.

It also renewed her mad desire to run into the forest, to find whatever it was that pulled at her. As she lay snuggled with several others for warmth, she finally admitted to herself what it was. It was the Compulsion. Somewhere out there in the dark forest there was an Elf who burned inside as she did. He had come from Kress, he had come for her.

The next day carried the slow-moving army and its followers away from Draton, for it was now lost from sight behind them. In the forest Arlon rejoiced as the queen and her people arrived. The Elves were now nearly three thousand strong. The odds had been cut to two or three to one.

They conferred for some time then orders were given, and warriors moved out. Arlon held half the forces in place and Tanis slipped away with the rest. They'd cross the open road ahead of the marching army in the night. By morning the Elves would command both sides of the roadway.

Ariel and her people settled down for the night, but she awakened early to find Freida staring into the fire. "You look troubled, my sister."

"I am. Ariel, what am I? What have I become?"

"Something disturbs you, Freida. Tell me."

"The dreams came upon me again in the night. He came to me again, the god smith, he who taught me to make the sword. He came wearing armor and carrying a blade such as I have never seen. 'I will stand at your side this day, my child,' he said. 'Together we will avenge our people, and then we will return to the forge. With this mark will you know I'm there beside you.'

"I felt a burning on my arm and awakened to find this." She moved her cloak aside and pushed up the sleeve of her tunic. She wore a new tattoo just below her shoulder. It was a sword crossed with a hammer and it glowed a dull red as though made of coals in the forge. "What am I now, Ariel?"

Queen Ariel held her hand over the tattoo and closed her eyes. A smile of delight slowly came to her face. "You are now the Princess Freida, my beloved sister, Blacksmith of Fugitive, beloved of the Dwarves and Orcs. You are Freida, daughter of the god smith, and, my darling sister, you have become mighty. You were tortured and tormented, but you are made of the god metal, and you have become unbreakable, undefeatable, just like your sword."

Ariel moved her hand to Freida's heart. "I feel the pain and rage within you, my sister. You will unleash that against our enemies this day, you will set free our people as we promised so long ago, and you will free yourself of the fear that haunts you.

"I set you free as promised, Freida, and now you must set the rest of them free. Go among them at the end of this day and when the next dawn arises I'll distract the leaders for you. When I do, set our people free, daughter of the god smith, send them to Elfhome, and then together we'll destroy our old enemy and return home to Fugitive."

Ariel smiled as she saw Freida slowly accept what she'd said. "As you desire, my Queen, my sister, so shall it be. This coming day we prepare, the next we strike with the fury of an angry god." Ariel gave her a gentle hug then slipped away to find Mearith.

The day passed slowly for Sayta, the call inside her ever holding her attention, urging her to run to the forest. By the end of day the trees were closer to the road, and because of that, he was nearer. She had managed to work her way slowly to the side of the column. The guards were close as well, but this position kept her as near as possible to the trees which hid that which she needed most, the one thing her very soul ached for.

As they settled down for the night, Sayta slowly ate her meager bowl of oshar and stared at the nearby trees. "Don't even think about it, slave," snarled a guard as he saw her moving forward. "You make a run for it, and I'll put a blade through your back." He pushed her roughly into the mass of slaves and glared at her.

As the guard held his focus on her, he didn't see what Sayta saw. Through the gloom a dozen shadowy figures slipped from the trees and into the mass of slaves. She was now pulled in a new direction, back into the press. He had come for her.

Moving toward that unknown pull, Sayta felt an unnatural joy swell up inside her. Her soul sang with a giddiness, and she began to hurry. Her world seemed to vanish in ecstasy as a figure stepped into her path and swept a cloak around her. She was pulled tightly to a hard muscled body, and she wept with the joy of it.

"Eat this, my beloved, it will give you strength." The voice was soft and gentle as something was pressed into her hands. The taste of the dried berry cake was like nothing she'd tasted before, and she ate greedily. "You're nearly starved, you poor soul," said that gentle voice.

A woman stood near and the power emanating from her caused others to move away from her in fear. This woman was no slave. When she spoke her voice commanded attention and obedience. "Olan, all is well?"

"It will be as soon as I can get her away from this accursed place, Lady."

"Soon, my friend. When the dawn comes." She turned to another. "Korath, spread the word. All must be ready when the morning comes." That one nodded then he and his companions spread out through the slaves, speaking to many who then spoke to others in turn.

The man in whose cloak Sayta cuddled spoke again as he pressed more of the magical food into her hand. "I am Olan, of the Queen's Guard. I've come to take you away to a safe place."

"My name is Sayta," she replied shyly. "I will happily go wherever you wish to take me."

"Then rest here against me. When the dawn comes we will go to the forest where our people are waiting."

She snuggled closer into his embrace. "That woman, is she the High Born Queen?"

"Allow me to introduce you, my love. This woman is Princess Freida, sister of Queen Ariel, and the master smith of Fugitive. Lady Freida, this is the light of my life, Sayta."

"I am well pleased to meet you, Satya. Rest now, for soon we will have to move swiftly. Already the light begins to break the sky."

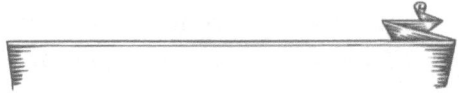

The Approaching Storm

Tanis and Eline worked diligently to get their troops ready. Their bows were slung across shoulders and long poles were chosen, long sturdy poles. These men they faced were clad in heavy armor, bows would be of little use. The idea was to draw them into the trees then unhorse them with the long poles. A man in heavy plate armor is no match for an Elf in the forest, especially if he's on foot.

Hundreds were ready with poles while near them lurked more with drawn blades. A man would be knocked from his horse, then attacked with sword and dagger. The lightning reflexes of the Elves combined with the hampering weight of the enemy's armor would tell the tale in the end.

As the sky lightened, the Reavers could be seen on the roadway, their light ponies prancing and ready for a fight. At the head of their column stood two huge war horses, Mearith's black stallion and the mighty Grimm. It was about to begin.

Eline grinned as she gently nudged Tanis. "Getting that old itch?"

"Indeed, my love. I'd far rather the Lady had let me lead the Reavers."

"You just want to start a fight."

Tanis laughed softly and hugged her shoulders. "How well you know me." Suddenly a horse broke from the group and raced towards the hills where Tanis was hidden. "Oh, oh, something's just gone sideways."

"As it all too often does," grinned Eline. "Let's greet the rider."

They stepped out of the trees and Kern soon skidded to a halt beside them. "Something's happened and they're doubling the guards on the slaves. The Queen and Lady Mearith are headed back that way. She commands that you lead the Reavers."

With a laugh Tanis leaped up behind Kern. "Eline, the troops are yours." With that they raced away, back to the fighters gathered in the road. A horse was soon produced for Tanis and he mounted, pulling his hood up to hide his face.

IN THE MASS OF SLAVES, Korath began to curse softly as he tried in vain to calm those nearest him. The word had spread like wildfire through the thousands of people. The Elf Queen had come, she was here to free them. She would magically appear and carry them away when the sun returned to the sky. The were all standing and milling about nervously.

"Lady, they could stampede at any moment," said Olan. "If they do hundreds will die in the crush and still many more on the blades of the guards. Even now the guards are being doubled."

"I know," replied Freida, as she saw the numbers of the guards increasing, forming a wall of armed men between them and the forest. "Korath, quickly now, spread the word, get them back so I have room to fight. Tell them we need to clear a path before they can run to the trees."

She continued to mutter to herself as the Queen's Guard tried to calm the excited slaves. "I hope those bloody mages have the portals ready. This is going to come apart any moment now." Even as she spoke she heard the war horns sound in the distance.

BACK IN THE TREES, hidden from the view of the army below, Drakkat was struggling to keep Rakka in check. "Easy, girl, be easy now."

"The waiting is making me crazy."

"I know, I know, but if we tip them off too soon all hell will break loose and the Queen will have our hides. Patience, girl, just a while longer."

At that point a mage approached. "We're ready. We can raise three portals; where do you want them?"

Drakkat turned and pointed to the clearing on the rise behind him. "There. We'll try to funnel them to you. There are thousands of them, can you hold the portals open long enough?"

"We can, but then we'll have to sleep for a week," she grinned. "The sun rises. We begin." With that she turned away, calling to her companions. As they began their chants Drakkat moved his people out to the edge of the tree line.

THE SUN WAS ABOUT TO top the hill and the queen was well away. Trelanth moved her horse up beside Tanis. "Shall I project your voice for you?"

"Please do," he grinned as he eased his horse forward. She smiled as she waited for the Reavers to fold her back into their ranks. She held her attention on him as they followed a hundred yards behind him.

Tanis walked his horse along the road toward the approaching army. The ranks of men at arms were just awakening when the posted guards sounded the horns. Swearing profusely the knights struggled into their armor then mounted the plunging horses their squires tried to hold steady for them. By the time they were mounted and formed up a single rider was almost within bowshot of their ranks.

The general forced his way through and approached the lone rider. "Halt where you are. Who are you, friend or foe?"

"That depends," came the reply. The voice was soft spoken, yet everyone in the entire army heard it clearly.

"What does that mean?" bellowed the general. "Explain yourself or die."

"My name is Tanis," replied the hooded rider as he swept back his hood. It was an Elf. Suddenly the men at arms were nervous, looking around furtively towards the trees on either side of the roadway. The Elf had approached them at the widest section of clear fields between Draton and Kress. What could he be up to?

"I'm a friend," Tanis went on, "if you drop your weapons and leave this field. Return to the lands to plant crops, accept the rule of her majesty, Queen Ariel. Do this and I'm your friend."

"And if we refuse you?" laughed the general. "What then?"

"Then you die here on this road. I will give you a few moments to discard your armor and leave this field, but your time for choosing grows late."

"Attack," roared the general as he urged his horse forward. Behind him his men readied their lances and moved to join him.

Tanis reeled as a wall of fear hit him, but it was gone in an instant. A Geni in mages robes fell from the saddle and the mounted men rode over the body as they picked up speed toward Tanis. They were barely halfway to him when the Reavers swept past at a gallop. Kern led half to the right and Tanis joined the rest on the left.

The riders on the smaller, swifter, horses sped toward the mounted knights then at the last moment split away. Arrows flew and a few men fell from the saddle, but these men were heavily armored. As the smaller horses sped away the mounted warriors gave chase. The Elves fled right into the trees with dozens of mounted men close behind.

As the heavier mounts entered the forest, long poles appeared and riders were swept from the saddle. Others tried to trample the Elves, but the Borni were long experienced at this kind of fighting. They easily avoided the horses and, leaping up behind the riders, pulled them from the saddle.

Out on the road, others watched as riderless horses began to return from the trees. Suddenly the Elvish riders came streaming out of the forest to attack. Again the mounted warriors turned to face them, but they swept aside, loosed arrows into the foot soldiers, then sped away towards the trees once again. Again they were pursued, with the same result.

WHILE THE MOUNTED KNIGHTS tried to deal with the elusive Reavers at the front of the army, mayhem had erupted back at the slave corrals.

"There are the war horns," said Korath. "Shall we give them a few minutes to have their attention diverted?"

"Yes indeed," replied Freida. The wolfish grin on her face made him shiver and the slaves moved away from her. "Olan, stay behind me until I cut a hole through them. Take her to the forest then help guard the mages."

"Yes, Lady. Come now, sweet Sayta. The Lady Freida will soon give us a path to freedom. Stay alert now. When she begins she will cast aside her cloak and tunic. Scoop them up and we'll follow her." He no sooner finished speaking when Freida shrugged out of her cloak and tunic, her sword leaping to her hand.

Terrified now, the slaves melted away from her as she marched toward the wall of guards. "You there, slave, what are you doing with that sword? Give that to me now."

"With extreme pleasure," she snarled then leaped at him. She screamed her battle challenge as the blade leaped forward, slicing the Orc in half. The back swing beheaded another guard. The guards surged toward her, and she released the rage within her. Her new tattoo glowed blood red as though on fire, and her fury was like pure madness, the rage of a goddess unleashed.

The guards fought and died as she waded through them. She was moving too fast for them to strike, her blows slew each as the god blade passed through armor, flesh and bone. Even as they tried to mass against her there was a wild scream of challenge. Drakkat and the Scratite Orcs burst from the trees and raced to her side.

A horse plowed through the melee then a half naked Orc woman leaped from the saddle. Nearly as wild as the raging Elf, she soon stood beside her friend. Side by side they slew all before them. The Scratite soon swept aside the rest of the guards and Korath led the first of the slaves through that hole to freedom.

The slaves ran to the forest where Elves waved them on, pointing them toward the glowing portals. "Through here. Through the portal. Quickly now." The mages urged them onward. The stream of escaping slaves grew into a river as the Orcs and Freida cleared away the opposition.

At length more foot soldiers came running to reinforce the guards. Freida was slowly getting pushed back when the war horse screamed. With a thunder of hooves that was enhanced by magic, Ariel charged from the trees. Even before she reached the battle Mearith's black sped past her, slamming into the foot soldiers, spreading them out, trampling them asunder, and creating panic.

And then Grimm hit the wall of fighting men. Still bellowing his challenge he reared and plunged, killing and maiming as he went, lashing out with iron shod hooves. Ariel sat easily as he danced beneath her, loosing arrow after arrow. The footmen broke and tried to flee into the ranks of men coming to help them.

Those left behind were faced with the mad fury of the god smith's daughter, and Freida slew them by the numbers. Rakka's arms grew heavy with fatigue as the day wore on, but Freida seemed not to tire. Rakka fought on.

The day was well along and there were still plenty of slaves trying make good their escape, but the former owners and townsfolk who had been marching behind tried to recapture them. Suddenly Ariel's massive charger was among them, and the slaves were soon abandoned.

Rakka's fatigue was beginning to tell and she took a slight wound. That enraged her enough to return to full power, but only for a few moments then she faltered and took another wound. "Ariel," shouted Freida as the queen rode by on her plunging charger. Ariel moved closer then Freida seized Rakka and tossed her up behind the queen.

"Come, Freida, our work is done here for now," shouted Ariel as she herded the last of the slaves on ahead of her.

"I still have more to do," replied the Princess, then shrieked as Mearith swept her up onto her horse as she galloped by.

"Save a few for tomorrow," Mearith laughed merrily as she carried the tired warrior into the trees. The Scratite and dozens of Elvish warriors closed the trail behind them. There was no real pursuit. The slaves were gone, hundreds of men at arms and camp followers lay dead. Those left alive were just thankful to see the demon Elf vanish from the field.

Ariel and Mearith dropped their passengers off by the portals then rode away toward the front. They found the battle there at a standstill. The army had taken up a defensive position, creating a circle the Elves couldn't penetrate.

Back by the portals Drakkat found Freida and Rakka leaning against each other and chewing on dried berry cakes. "Did we get them all?" asked Freida.

"Most of them," grunted Drakkat as he lowered himself to the ground beside Rakka. "We lost a few dozen. Some were trampled in the stampede; others were brought down by the guards and the rabble of camp followers. However, I'd say we got the best part of them free. Let's ask the mage."

They looked up to see one of the mages walking toward them. "My Lady Freida," she said as she knelt.

"Sit woman, sit and rest," replied Freida as she gently pulled the woman down beside her. "Kneel to my sister and her lady, but never me. Now, tell me how we fared this day."

The woman sighed and gave Freida a smile of gratitude as she relaxed. "Lady, a full eight thousand Elves passed through the portals this day. Lady, we could not imagine so many of the folk had survived, but now ..."

"So we did well," grinned Freida. "Now, my friend, you have a decision to make."

"I do?"

"You're exhausted, as are your companions. Will you now return to Elfhome to assist the king and his people as they work with the newly freed, or will you remain here this night to guard the Princess as she gets some much needed rest?"

The woman grinned her delight. "We will, of course, remain to serve the royal house as needed, Lady."

"Then I command you to get some rest as Rakka and I plan to do. Drakkat can keep the watch, he's had little enough to do this day."

His great bellow of laughter echoed through the forest. With a grin he rose to his feet. "Aye, Lady Blacksmith, get some rest, you too Rakka. You both fought like demons this day. The Scratite will keep the watch this night.

"Oh, what should we do with Olan? He's as useless as a Geni with that woman attached to his side." Olan and Sayta were sitting close by and he shook his fist at Drakkat who matched his grin.

"If he's of little use, then let him rest," chuckled Freida. "We'll let the queen decide his fate."

Sayta looked concerned, but he smiled and cuddled her closer. "Do not fear, my love, they're friends and they tease us, nothing more. Relax now and sleep, tomorrow will bring new wonders."

AHEAD ALONG THE ROAD Tanis called for Mary and Garret. They found him beside a campfire, staring thoughtfully at the flames, Eline at his side. "You sent for us, Lord Tanis?"

"Yes, Ellen. Come, sit. It appears that we have a standoff with the army for the moment. We thinned them out a bit, and they still outnumber us, but I don't think we all need to be here. I've left a few folks back at the gates of Kress, but, too few of them to be helpful.

"Here's what I'd like you folks to do. I'd like you to take your people back to the gates of Kress, see how many recruits you can get for your clan, or, at the very least, help to feed them if you can."

"Of course," replied Ellen. "I know Mary would far rather go hunting than fight a war. Do you want to keep Brak with you?"

"No, keep your people together. Ellen, if Kress sends out relief fighters to help this army, send the Elves to me with warning, but you stay back to help the refugees. Warn them to stay clear of the open roads until this army has been dealt with."

"You're trying to keep as many farmers alive as possible," said Garret. "You don't need them, why bother?"

"Garret, we displaced those people because we had no other option. The queen wants allies among the humans and Orcs. The idea isn't to eliminate everybody who isn't an Elf, the idea is to find a way we can all live together, share the land, and prosper in peace. We brought great hardship upon those folk, now I'd like to help lighten their load as much as I can. Unfortunately, I have a war to fight right now. We Elves are now many, but your folk aren't. I want you to survive. Keep Brak with you, for he may be the last of his kind in these lands."

Garret nodded as he and Ellen rose then departed back to their own camp.

Eline snuggled closer to Tanis, laying her head on his shoulder. "I know how you hurt, my love."

"Mmm?"

"Your heart hurts, you burn with feelings of guilt. You shouldn't, Tanis."

"Why should I not? My sweet Eline, this is my doing. I'm the one who devised this plan, I led the Reavers as we drove the people from their homes, made refugees of them."

She sighed and squeezed his hand. "You led the fighters who set free the slaves who labored unto death on those farms. You delivered unto the masters but a small taste of what they have visited on our people.

"Look now at Ellen and Garret, their people. Look at Mary, she no longer depends on slaves, but instead has embraced her former slave as an equal and as a bonded companion. Is this not what we set out to accomplish? My love, the birth was painful, but the child of the future has been born in those people you just sent to safety.

"Besides, was not the queen and her lady companion, as well as the rest of her advisers, there when the plan was hatched?"

"I suppose."

"What bothers you is that you took joy in what we did, yes?"

"You know me too well."

"Tanis, it was natural for you to enjoy returning some of the pain you'd endured. We aren't gods, my love, we're all flawed, and sadly, many of us were broken. All we can do is take each day as it comes and try to live that day with honor."

Tanis gave her a gentle squeeze and chuckled. "You've been talking to Drakkat again. Alright, my love, I'll stop brooding now. So, how are we going to crack open that wall of defense they've thrown up?"

"That's a task for the queen to decide," she replied.

"Then advise me," said Ariel as she appeared beside their fire and sank to the ground. They both tried to scramble up to a kneeling position, but she waved them back down. "Relax, dear friends, relax. I was serious, advise me. Eline?"

"Lady, we could do as we've done all winter," said Eline as Mearith joined them.

Mearith grinned. "You mean keep them bottled up until they eat all the food and wallow in their own crap?"

"Yes, Lady. Sooner or later they'll have to break formation, and when they do ..."

"I like it," said Mearith. "Ariel?"

"Yes, I believe this to be the right course of action, but there are problems."

Mearith nodded. "Tanis has already sent reinforcements back to Kress. We'll have plenty of warning if trouble comes from that quarter. Are you thinking about Draton and Elb?"

"I am. It's early in the year yet for the sea rovers to come, so I've been told, but ..."

"But you want to send some people back to burn the cities to the ground so the sea rovers can't gain an easy foothold in our lands, yes?"

"Yes, my love, that's what I'd like to do. Tanis, what think you?"

"Forgive me, my queen, but I don't like it."

"Oh? Why not?"

"Lady, Arlaith has often spoken of these things. The pirates come, raid all along the coast, but the men at arms from Draton and Elb have always kept them in check. If we burn those cities they'll have free rein to raid much further inland. If they come and find the walls still standing, it will give them pause."

"Yes, for a short time, but will they not then inhabit those cities and thus gain a foothold on our lands?"

"Perhaps, Lady, but we could deal with them then as we have with those places even now."

"So, one battle at a time? Leave future struggles until they appear? Is this the advice you give me?" asked Ariel, a merry twinkle in her eye.

"It is, my queen," he grinned sheepishly.

"From the mouths of babes comes wisdom aplenty," grinned Mearith as she lightly punched his arm. "Lord Arlon has advised the same," smiled Ariel, but I wanted to get your take on it before making the final decision. So be it, we leave the coast to its fate for now and focus on defeating those before us.

"Tanis, each morning return to the enemy with the offer of joining our allies if they drop weapons and leave the field. Sooner or later they will begin to accept the offer, the army will fall apart. When that happens they will try something desperate.

"Get some rest now. Come, Mearith my heart, we still have more campfires to visit, and the night grows old." With that Ariel rose and they left Tanis and Eline to their fire and their thoughts.

As the sun rose the next morning the alarm was sounded once again. Again the men at arms leaped from their blankets to hastily mount plunging horses. The foot soldiers formed up and they waited. Once again a lone hooded rider faced them. Once again he spoke, his voice magically enhanced to reach all ears in the massed people in the open road.

"Hear me, soldiers of the Geni. Yesterday you refused my offer of freedom and alliance with the Elves. Our Lady Ariel, Queen of all Elves, directs me to offer you the choice a second time.

"Yesterday you refused me and hundreds of you perished in field and forest, your slaves were taken, and you faced the fury of the Lady Blacksmith. You have yet to face the magic of the High Born Queen reborn. Pray you never do.

"So, we come to it. Lay down your weapons, strip off your armor and return the way you came, no hand will be raised against you. Refuse me and die where you stand, for this army will go no further along this road."

"You think not, you accursed Elf?" roared the Geni leader. "You think not? Your stupid tricks will not avail you this day. The army moves on."

He barked an order and reluctantly, the army began to move. Tanis signaled and the Reavers thundered past him. He joined the column that split to the left. As they raced towards the army, the knights were suddenly surrounded by a defensive wall of foot soldiers holding up shields.

Eline, Tanis, and Kern had devised a plan in case such a thing happened. The Riders swept past the mounted men and foot soldiers. They loosed their arrows into the men defending the supply wagons. Just as the arrows reached the target, they burst into flames. With cries of protest, men and Orcs ran to rescue the burning wagons.

The Reavers wheeled around and raced back, loosing arrows at the men trying to quench the fires. This time the mounted knights attacked. As though driven by a single mind the Elves swept away towards the forest, holding their swift ponies back to give the charging knights hope they might actually catch up.

As the day before, the Reavers disappeared into the trees where there were Elves waiting with long poles to unhorse the pursuing knights. There were sounds of battle, screams of challenge and howls of pain. Nervously the army on the road waited. One by one the riderless horses began to return from the trees on both sides of the road.

As the day wore on, this was repeated twice more. It was clear now, the heavy horses had no chance to catch the smaller swifter forest ponies. There were barely a hundred mounted knights left and they knew their only hope for survival was to remain on the road.

Their long lances were chopped up for firewood that night. They would remain in the open where their armor could protect them. If the Elves wanted to close with them they'd have to come out of the trees and fight. Their morale sank as it became apparent the Elves had managed to destroy over half the food supplies.

The next morning dawned and again the horns sounded. Again there was a lone rider facing them on the road. This time they didn't wait for him to speak. Several bolts of energy lanced out at him, but the rider shrugged them off. Something was different this time. Horrified the Geni realized the five mages had fallen to the ground, dead.

The new rider was mounted on a gigantic gray warhorse. The hood was pushed back to reveal a woman's face. When she spoke her voice carried easily to all. "I am Ariel, the Queen Arisen. We have taken your slaves and set them free. When next you see them they will be warriors driving blades through your black hearts.

"We took your slaves, we slew your knights, and my sister, she who wields the god blade, slew your footmen by the numbers. We destroyed your food supplies, and you have advanced not one foot.

"I come to offer you this. All Geni and those who would continue to serve them, turn your steps south, return to the lands of your former home and pray I have no cause to pursue you there.

"Those of you who would remain in these lands, cast aside your armor and weapons. Walk away and return to the fields and farms that were destroyed. Rebuild them, become our allies, and we will not hinder you, we will help you where we can.

"People of the camp followers and refugees from the city gates, we offer you the same, return to the fields and farms as our allies. We won't hinder you and will assist you where we can. I grant you time to decide. When the sun reaches its highest point of rise this day we'll assume your decision has been made. The offer will not be made again."

With that she pulled her hood back over her face and turned her horse toward the trees. Twenty riders suddenly burst forth to pursue her, but they were cut off by a hundred riders on swift ponies. The mounted men ignored them and continued their attack, if they could manage to kill her the Elves would melt away.

Suddenly she wheeled the big gray and it screamed a challenge as it leaped at the oncoming knights. They came with drawn sword as they'd burned the lances the night before. Another war horse charged from the trees and raced toward them. Together they slammed into the pursuing riders.

The battle was swift and furious. The queen's horse reared and lashed out with deadly effect while her bow sang. Their armor was no protection from her, and they fell from the saddle with arrows piercing their hearts.

Mearith weaved among the rest, her blades leaving a trail of empty saddles behind her. The few who turned back to flee were cut down by the queen's bow. While that battle raged the army had surged forward to help, but they were swarmed by the riders on the lighter horses.

That's when disaster struck the army. With all eyes focused on the attempt to catch the Elf Queen, Eline led her warriors out into the field. Before anyone realized what was happening a thousand Elvish warriors were attacking their flank.

Full half the remaining footmen fell before they fully realized they were in danger. The Elves wore only leather armor, but they were unnaturally strong and fast. As the foot soldiers turned to fight, Arlon led his warriors onto the field.

As one the camp followers and refugees fled the madness. The Queen's voice carried easily to all as she spoke their doom. "Kill them all, let none survive this day." That pronouncement was followed by a wild scream of challenge as mounted Orcs sped from the trees led by a half naked Elf wielding a shining sword. She leaped from the saddle to land amid a cluster of armed footmen. An Orc woman was soon at her side.

"Why the three hells won't you ever wait for me?" shouted Rakka as she waded into the melee.

"No time, girl, no time," Freida shouted in reply. "There's work to be done."

The battle raged well into the afternoon, but the end was in sight. The camp followers had abandoned the field, fleeing for their lives. Some of the foot soldiers cast aside their weapons and ran. To their great surprise the Elves ignored them, letting them go. When the sun began to set, the vast army of the Geni was no more. The Elves left the field and returned to the forest. Slowly, some of those who'd fled returned to loot the bodies.

Beginning of the End

As the battle ended and the sun set Ariel made her way to a campsite in the forest. After rubbing down her horse, she sent for her advisers, and her sister as well. Slowly they drifted together, and darkness was fully on the lands by the time they had all gathered. They sat in silence, waiting for the queen to speak first.

With a sigh, Ariel tore her gaze from the flames and faced her people. "Arlon, of your people, how many dead, how many wounds?"

"Sixty-seven dead, two hundred wounds, none fatal so I'm told, my Queen."

"Tanis?"

"Three Reavers dead, nine wounds, none fatal, Lady. Eline, how fared our troops?"

Eline nodded. "Thirty-two dead, seven wounds that will not heal, and seventy more that are not fatal."

"Then, by some favor of the gods, we came away almost unscathed," said Arlon.

"A hundred dead and three hundred wounds make you happy, Arlon?" asked Ariel.

Mearith patted her shoulder. "Easy, my delight. Be easy. Arlon recalls our losses on the plains of Elanda before the breaking of the world. In those battles we lost hundreds of thousands and saw too few victories.

"This time we again fought a force of superior numbers, but we destroyed them with relatively few losses. Ariel, we set free thousands of slaves and destroyed the only army in the land that could oppose us to any extent. Rejoice, my delight, it is fatigue that weighs on your heart now, nothing more."

The queen squeezed Mearith's hand and gave a wan smile. She nodded then turned to Drakkat. "How fared the Scratite, old friend?"

"One dead, the rest carry a few scratches of no consequences," he grunted in reply. "The Princess Freida's Guard has fared better than we had a right to expect." Freida grinned and lightly punched his arm.

"All is well with you, my sister?" asked Ariel.

"It is. Ariel, we did it, as promised, we set them free. So many they were. I've never seen so many gathered in one place. When we moved among them they were packed so tightly together the stench of the oshar was overpowering. So many. I hope King Evenseth can cope with so many."

Trelanth chuckled at that. "My uncle says they're somewhat overwhelmed, but will manage. The great forest of Narthwood, however rejoices with the return of so many Elves."

"Then I guess all is well," sighed Ariel as she leaned against Mearith's shoulder. "When the sun returns to the sky let's find the remains of our fallen and return their spirits to the forest. I only wish there was something that could be done for those who won't recover from their wounds."

"There is," said a soft voice from the edge of the group. Ariel looked to see who had spoken. It was Sayta who sat cuddled in Olan's arms.

"Come closer," said Ariel, "speak to me of your meaning." Satya rose, approached, and knelt, but Ariel patted the ground beside her. "Sit beside me and speak of these things."

"Great Queen, as long as I can remember I have tended to the aged and dying of the family that owned me, and they were many, each in turn passing into the next world. I learned that, as a person becomes aware, and accepts that the end draws near, the nearness of a long time friend, family member, or even a stranger brings great comfort. Lady, if a friend of each could be free to sit the final watch with the passing, it would greatly ease that final step across the divide and into the next life."

"You are certain of this?"

"I am, Lady. I have seen it many times."

Ariel looked thoughtful for several moments then turned her attention back to the woman beside her. "Sayta, I have a great favor to ask of you, you and your companion."

"Of course, Lady, anything at all. Anything. Olan?"

"Olan, you well know that Randall grows more feeble with age," said Ariel. "You were ever my eyes and ears in Fugitive, and I would have that again. Also I would have Sayta's skills to tend Randall as needs arise, and I would have you, his long time trusted friend, ever at his side as his time approaches.

"This is what I beg of you. Will you return to my home and remain there to ease my friend and mentor's passing from this world to the next? Olan, I need this now more than I need a warrior. Will you do this for me?"

"With a happy heart, my Queen," replied Olan. "It will be easier for me to protect my Sayta there."

"My queen, you have made the joy in my heart possible, I will ever do anything you ask of me," said Sayta. "I would be honored to attend to your friend."

"Thank you both," sighed Ariel. "I am at peace with this now. Once we have laid our fallen to rest on the morrow I will create a portal to Fugitive for you.

"Once Olan and Sayta are on their way the rest of us will march to Kress. It's well past time to make an end of this and begin the process of rebuilding. We destroy Kress then march on Shotar to finish it."

Ariel was leaning heavily against Mearith and her voice had grown soft, barely audible. "My treasure," said Mearith, "since we first sighted the army you have rested little and accomplished much. While others rested you went from camp to camp, from fire to fire, speaking to each in turn. Now it's your turn to rest. Snuggle down here now and I'll watch over you as you sleep."

As Mearith settled Ariel under her cloak she gave Trelanth a knowing nod. Trelanth winked and passed her hand lightly over Ariel's forehead. Ariel giggled as she felt the tingle of the magic then drew a deep breath and released herself to the land of dreams. Mearith gave Trelanth a smile of thanks then closed her own eyes.

IN FAR AWAY SHOTAR the king swallowed hard, his face ashen, his hands trembling, as he faced the royal mage. "You are certain of this? This isn't some illusion she's shown you to frighten us."

"No, Sire, this is no illusion. She dropped all masking spells as soon as she reached the army. Sire, they're all dead. The mages, the knights, and the foot soldiers, all dead. The people have fled and the cities of Elb and Draton are cold and empty.

"Sire, she has destroyed them all and will now march on Kress. Kress will surely fall, and then she'll come for us. Shotar will be the last to fall, but fall it surely will."

"So there is but one chance left," said the armed man beside the throne, the king's brother. "She marches against Kress. Magdan has fallen so that road will be empty of Elves. We must flee to the south, take the road past Magdan, on to empty Elb, and from there along the coast to the safety of our ancient home."

"That place is hot and barren," sighed the king. "Can we even survive there?"

"Our ancestors managed it. I'd rather take my chances there than here against the Witch of Elanda and her hordes."

"Agreed, my brother, agreed. The task of preparing for the journey is yours. Be swift, for time is short. Make sure to bring every slave you can find. We'll need them on the journey and when we reach the south lands."

The soldier hurried away, and the king turned back to the mage. "Prepare your people, we'll have great need of your skills on the road to our ancient home."

The mage bowed and backed from the room then turned and hurried away. "Not my ancient home," he muttered as he ran. He burst into the mage tower, calling for his assistant. "Come, the time is upon us. We go now before that inbred fool gets us killed. By all the gods, he has no hope at all of reaching the south alive. She'll catch him and make an example of him. Quickly now, help me get this portal up."

ARIEL AND HER ARMY were on the march at break of day, but so was the king in Shotar. Lora was summoned early. "Lora, come, something is afoot within the city walls."

"What is it, Bralin?" she asked as she rose gracefully to her feet.

"I know not, but there is a great clatter near the gates. The refugees are massing, for they believe food will be forthcoming," replied Bralin.

"I doubt that," said Lora. She gave a piercing whistle and her warriors soon appeared at her side. Silently she led them toward the edge of the trees.

The Elves has barely arrived when the gates swung open and mounted men at arms rode out, slashing at the refugees with their swords and maces. Once the rabble had been driven back the rest of the procession appeared. First came the king, heavily guarded, followed by the rest of the Geni. Behind the hundreds of Geni came the slaves, nearly two thousand strong, and with them, many wagons of supplies.

The procession was still pouring from the gates when Lora turned to the man beside her. "Bralin, the queen engages the enemy on the road somewhere toward Draton. Find her, swiftly as you can. She must know of this. They're taking the road to Magdan." She'd barely finished speaking when he vanished into the trees.

"Lora, they're still coming out. What do you think they're up to?"

"Obviously they're aware of the battles on the road to the sea. My guess is the queen has been successful and they know there is no help coming. They're fleeing before Lady Ariel can get here to destroy them."

"They'll reach the town of Argar well before Bralin can reach the queen, Lora. You know they will."

"Yes, but we will reach Argar first. Come." With that she turned and sped through the forest, her warriors following close behind. While the city of Shotar slowly emptied of its people, the Elves ran well ahead of them.

With no slaves or wagons to weight them down, Lora and her fifty easily out distanced the Geni. Five days later they arrived to find the town prospering under the guidance of a human girl who seemed to be in command of the Elves there.

The day was well along when they came streaming out of the forest and into the fields of Argar. The alarm was sounded, then Julie was called to the Inn. She arrived to find Arlaith with another Elf. This one looked exhausted.

"Julie, my love, this woman is Lora. She has brought us dire news indeed."

"Is our doom upon us this moment?" asked the girl.

"You have a couple of days yet," grinned Lora.

"Good, then you have time to rest. Someone bring her food and see that her companions get food as well."

"It's already being done, Julie," replied an older woman as she set a bowl of stew before Lora.

"Excellent, Maggie you're the best. All right, Lora. What's coming for us and how long do we have to prepare?"

"Can you tell me how it is you came to be in command here?" asked Lora.

"Chain of command," smiled Julie. "The queen told Lord Tanis to garrison Magdan when we captured it. He in turn gave the command to Arlaith who insisted I do it. We burned Magdan to the ground and retreated here where the headman promptly retired and made me take her job. All I ever wanted was a warm woman to cuddle with, but the price was higher than I expected."

Lora laughed heartily at that. "Those who have leadership thrust upon them are often the best leaders," she said. "Sadly, girl, your time is short. The Geni have left Shotar en mass. They come with near five hundred men at arms and thousands of slaves as well as whatever camp followers march with them. We didn't wait to count them all, but raced here to give you fair warning."

"How long do we have?"

"They'll be here in three days or less."

Lora was startled at how fast the girl leaped to action. "Arlaith, sound the alarm, quickly now. Lora, rest, but on the morrow we'll need your help."

"You'll have it," replied Lora as Arlaith stepped through the door and blew a long blast on a war horn. She was speaking to thin air for Julie had already left the building. Lora went to the door to watch as the people swiftly gathered in the square.

A big Orc stepped close and tossed Julie up onto his shoulders. She windmilled her arms for a moment to get her balance then addressed the gathered townsfolk. "Good people of Argar, our doom is nearly upon us. The Geni have fled Shotar, and march this way with their army and thousands of slaves."

"They'll kill us all, they'll steal everything, burn us out. Julie, what will we do?"

She let them clamor for a few minutes then called out again. "Hear me, good people, friends and family, hear me. The Geni may come, but they will gain not one scrap from Argar. We'll take everything that will move, all the food, livestock, weapons, and other resources. Everything we'll need to rebuild we will take from this place, and then we'll burn it to the ground. Not one scrap of food nor a single stick of firewood will the Geni find.

"We'll flee into the forest until they pass us by on their trek to the south. The Elves will help us, but they have another task, so we must do as much of this as we can by ourselves. Rest this night, then on the morrow we pack up and move on. We'll vanish into the forest and the Geni will have no idea where we've gone."

"They'll know," cried out a frightened woman. "They'll use magic to find us."

"That matters not," replied Julie. "People, the Geni flee the lands. They fear the Elf Queen and they flee from her wrath. Even if they spy us out they dare not take the time to run us down. She could fall upon them at any moment, and they know this. No, we'll be safe in the forest, and once they've passed us by, we will return and rebuild. Never again will we have to live in fear of the Geni. Rest now, my brothers and sisters, we march with the rising sun."

Julie hopped down from the Orc's shoulders, gave him a friendly pat in the back then returned to the inn. Arlaith was with her, and they rejoined Lora at the table. "Arlaith, my beloved, both you and Lora command fifty warriors. Which of you is to command them all?"

"Lora," replied Arlaith. "She is of the Borni and far more experienced than I."

"Actually, grinned Lora, "the most able leader in the room seems to be a human. Lord Julie, you're in command here, Arlaith is your second, and I lead the fifty. Tell me what you need of us."

Julie sighed and blushed deeply. Command was never a thing she desired, but seemed a natural for it when it was thrust upon her. "All right, I need Arlaith and her people to find us suitable campsites and help us reach them. I need you and yours to keep an eye on the enemy, delay them if you can, but take no chances. They will pass us by, for they have not the time to stay and fight."

Later, as she lay in Arlaith's arms, Julie spoke softly. "My love, how is it that a Borni warrior, several thousand years old, would so readily obey the commands of a human girl barely grown to womanhood?"

"It's the wisdom of the Elf, my cuddle bunny," replied Arlaith. "Lora needs to defend these people by the Queen's desire. She could easily see that they all look to you for direction. If she tried to seize command it could take far too long to get things moving the right way, and many folk might not be prepared to listen. By putting you in command the people hurry to obey because they trust you to lead them.

"In this way they will all be safely in the forest well before the Geni arrive, and thus, the queen's wish is granted. It's not about who's in control for the Elf, sweetie, it's about how to get the task accomplished with the least resistance."

"I feel so used and taken advantage of," giggled Julie.

"Not yet, sweet bunny, just let me squirm around here a bit and ..."

"Arlaith!"

"Yes, my precious?"

"Hurry up."

The next day dawned bright and sunny, but the people were already awake and working. Wagons were soon loaded with goods and supplies. Money and small treasures were buried or hidden in cellars, tools and other equipment stored in wagons or carried on pack horses. The elders and infirm were also put on horses or in wagons and taken to the forest.

As the day wore on the wagons made several trips to the trees and the camps hidden therein. By the end of day the once prosperous and sprawling town of Argar was empty. An old Orc convinced Julie to wait before setting the fires. He wanted to wait until the Geni would be certain to see the smoke rising. It would help to demoralize them further.

The campfires crackled cheerily, the people gathered round them, chatting and speculating on what would happen when the Geni arrived. Julie and Arlaith went from fire to fire, speaking with the folk gathered there, reassuring and comforting them as best they could.

Next morning Arlaith led her fifty Elves back to Argar and lit the fires. By the time the sun was well up the flames rose up sending smoke high into the clear air.

Riding at the head of the procession, the Geni king topped a small rise and saw the smoke in the distance. With a howl of denial he turned to his brother and pointed. That soldier barked a command and a hundred men at arms followed him as he rode ahead to see the cause of the rising smoke.

The king continued to curse and swear. He needed supplies and had hoped to get them at Argar. He already knew Magdan had been razed to the ground, but also knew the town of Argar prospered. That fire could only mean one thing. The Witch of Elanda had cut him off and caught him in the open with barely five hundred fighters, and not a single mage of any skill at all.

He was still cursing as his brother returned. "The town is ablaze, my king. There'll be no aid for us there. We saw a small group of Elves, but they fled into the forest at our approach. Rather than ride into an ambush we didn't follow them, but returned to you. What are your commands."

The king was trembling with fear. "What do you suggest?"

"We have no choice, and if she attacks we have little chance. I suggest we push onward as fast as we can. With luck that small band of Elves is all there are in the area. She knew of the army out of Drayton. She and her main force should be on that road. We should run while we can."

The king began to protest. "The riders can move faster, but not the slaves. How can we push them harder than we already are?"

The soldier leaned closer. "My brother, we know there are Elves in the forest, for each night they kill a few of our guards and steal a few slaves. There cannot be many of them because they haven't attacked us openly. I suggest we pick up the pace and dump out half the slaves. The Elves will be too busy gathering them up to hinder us.

"Leave them the old, too young, sick or pregnant, any infirm, keeping only the strongest, the most likely to survive the hard march to the southlands."

"And our people?"

"The same. You know as well as I the Witch of Elanda will come for us. We need to fly. The strong will survive to rebuild our people in the south. Perhaps there they can regain their former glory and return to crush the Elves."

The king fairly shook with fear atop his charger. "Make it happen, my brother. Do what you must, but get us moving." So saying he urged his horse ahead, his personal guard staying close behind him.

His brother began barking orders. From the trees the Elves watched as the procession suddenly began to spread out. Horses were being whipped up and slaves were being culled from the masses. As the slaves ran any who couldn't keep up were left behind to stand bewildered on the road as the long column fled into the distance.

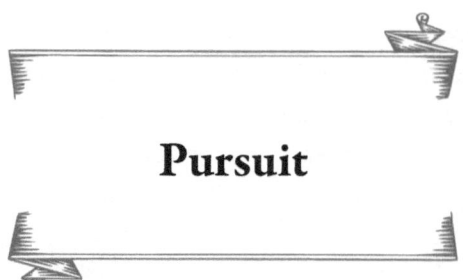

Pursuit

Well before the king of the Geni saw the smoke of Argar's fires an exhausted Elf reached the camp of those watching the gates of Kress. He sat beside the campfire, drinking deeply of the sweet forest air and relating his message. As soon as the news passed his lips another left the camp at a dead run, heading for the queen's army on the road to Draton. Two days later he found them marching toward Kress.

The runner had long since abandoned the forest for easier traveling on the open road. Sighting the riders approaching, he stopped and sank to the ground, gasping for breath. They had nearly reached him before he regained his feet and approached, kneeling before the queen.

"Queen Ariel, I bring dire news."

She was off the horse in a flash, raising him to his feet. A wave of her arm brought her advisers to her side. "Breathe now, my friend, breathe. Tell us your news."

"Lady, the Geni have abandoned Shotar. They march south on the road to Elb with five hundred men at arms and over two thousand slaves as well as various civilians. The king himself leads them."

"Argar," gasped Tanis. "It lies right in his path and has no defense."

Ariel spun around to face her people. "Arlon, take your warriors to Kress and deal with that. Tanis, we make for Agar. You can move faster with the Reavers. Take them and go, the rest of us will catch up as quickly as we can."

"There's more, Lady," said the messenger. Ariel turned back to him. "The human forest runners led by Tek have already abandoned the gates of Kress and are marching to Argar. The giant goes with them."

"They're no match for mounted men at arms," said Ariel, "Tanis ..."

"He's already in the forest, my delight," said Mearith.

"And so should we be, let's go." Ariel leaped back to the saddle while Arlon was bawling orders. The Elves swiftly sorted themselves out, half staying on the road to Kress while the rest followed the Reavers into the trees. They would do their best, but she knew Tanis and the Reavers, riding their swift forest ponies, would arrive well before the rest.

It took Tanis days to cross the forest to the road through Argar. He arrived to find Argar burned to the ground and the Geni camped in the open road near the ruins.

Tek and Mary led their people through the trees as fast as they could. Several detoured to where they'd left their elders and children. The best archers and the giant continued on. They found the camp of the Argar people a day before Tanis arrived.

"By now the queen is aware," said Tek as they all sat around the fire, exchanging news. "What are your orders, Lora?"

Lora just chuckled. "Sorry Tek, but I lost my job. Julie's in command here. What do you think, Lord Julie, do we attack them or not?"

"Not yet," replied Julie. "For now we ..." An Elf burst into the camp and ran straight to her.

"Lord Julie, the Geni are moving faster. They've left dozens of slaves on the road and others as well."

"Catch your breath," smiled Julie as she patted his shoulder. "Arlaith, Lora, is this a trap, do you think?"

"No, I don't think so," replied Lora. Arlaith agreed.

"Garret, you served in that city, what think you, trap?"

"No, Julie, I think they're running. I'll bet they've learned the queen is aware of them now and they're running."

"Then we'll let the queen deal with them. Lora, take whoever you need, find those lost and abandoned slaves and bring them here. Arlaith, take your warriors and watch the Geni. Gather up any more slaves they leave on the road. We are too few to fight them, but we can offer aid to those they leave behind."

"What of the slower Geni, the Orcs and humans that have been left behind?" asked Arlaith, a twinkle in her eye.

"Ignore them, just bring me the slaves. If those others attempt to follow you, discourage them."

"By your command, Lord Julie," grinned Arlaith as she winked at Lora.

"Go, both of you. Go tease someone else," laughed Julie. "Tek, Garret, our numbers are growing at an alarming rate. Might I prevail upon your folk to go hunting?"

"Mary's already gone out," grinned Tek. "I'll send a few more. The rest can stay with Ellen and Garret to guard the camp."

Julie smiled her thanks as he rose and trotted away.

Tanis stood gazing at the Geni encampment that sat near the burned out ruins of Argar. A terrible rage gripped him, and he fought for control. Eline gently squeezed his arm. "Easy, my love, be easy. Let the rage take control and disaster will follow it. I swear we will avenge them."

"Don't mourn the dead just yet," said Kern, who sat atop his horse near them. "I see Elves slipping about near the Geni camp. I think we should ask them exactly what happened here." He touched his heels to the horse which leaped away.

Fighting to gain control of the rage, Tanis watched as Kern raced toward the Geni. He was near the guard post when he called out and turned the horse aside, a shadow leaping to the animal's back behind him. Without a pause in the beast's stride, they returned to Tanis at the edge of the forest where Kern's passenger hopped lightly to the ground and saluted.

"Greetings, my Lord Tanis."

"Arlaith. I'm happy to see you're here and still alive. What can you tell me about what has happened. How many managed to survive?"

"All survived, my Lord. As ordered, we burned Magdan and proceeded to Argar. The headman there had taken a bad fall and gave over the task to my Julie. When word reached us of the Geni on the march, Julie ordered all to take what they could carry into the forest then we burned Argar to the ground so the Geni would gain nothing of value there.

"The people of Argar are camped a ways from here, and Ellen's forest runners have joined them. All are quite safe. The Geni have begun to hurry, and so have abandoned many slaves by the roadside, others of their own kind as well.

"Julie has Lora and her people gathering up the slaves and taking them to her in the camp. I and mine are picking off the camp guards and stealing as many horses as we can. The idea is to slow them down until the forces of the Queen can get here."

Tanis was shaking now with the power of the emotion that gripped him. "Alive? They're alive?"

"Yes, Lord Tanis, they're all alive."

"Julie did this?"

"She did. I seem to have bonded with a bossy woman," grinned Arlaith.

"Take me to them, Arlaith. "Eline, make camp here, I'll be back as soon as I've ..."

"Go, my love, see for yourself they're safe then return to us. When the sun rises the Reavers will be ready to go to war," said Eline, gripping his shoulder tightly. He kissed her lightly then set out with Arlaith.

They left the trees then trotted along the edge of the open fields until they reached the trail to the human's camp. "Julie," called Arlaith, "I've brought a visitor."

The girl rose easily from the fire, then stopped as she recognized the man with Arlaith. "Lord Tanis, I ..."

She'd started to kneel, but Arlaith caught her arm and stopped her. "Like this, love," smiled Arlaith as she curled Julie's hand into a fist and placed it at her shoulder.

Grinning broadly, Tanis returned the salute then seized Julie in a bear hug. "I owe you more than you know, woman," he said as he set her down. "I arrived to find Argar burned, and the Geni camped at the ashes. I thought them all dead, but you've kept them alive."

"Alive but barely," spoke up an old Orc nearby. "This woman is a hard task master, Sir. First she has us build more barns then a few days later she burns them down. Now I expect she'll be wanting us to build them back up again."

He was grinning at Julie who matched his grin. "Parr, I have to keep you busy or who knows what mischief you'd get up to."

"Arlaith says you've recovered abandoned slaves," said Tanis.

"Yes, Lora has brought them here and we're doing our best to help them adjust," replied Julie.

"Call your people back, Julie," said Tanis. "Rest them. You've done wonderfully and deserve some rest. Tomorrow the Reavers will harry the Geni, and by the next day the queen and her army should arrive to finish the task. When all is done we'll do what we can to help you rebuild." He patted her shoulder, winked at Arlaith, then left the camp at a run.

Dawn came and the Geni were already up and on the move. By the time the sun rose over the horizon the full column was in motion. And then they saw the lone rider, sitting atop his horse, directly in their path. His face was hidden within a hood, but his presence brought a strong sense of foreboding to the king.

The king, surrounded by a dozen armed men rode forward toward the stranger, but, as they neared he held up a hand to stop them. "That's close enough."

No one had spoken to king Kratac in that tone since the death of his father, yet that voice spoke with command and authority. He stopped his horse and his guard. "Who are you, what do you want? How dare you speak to me thus?"

"My name is Tanis, known as Lord Tanis, a title I earned when I was given command of a thousand warriors. In this time and place I speak for Queen Ariel. Listen carefully. Release all your slaves to me and you may continue your journey to the lands of the south unhindered. Give me all the slaves and my people will escort you to the border lands."

"And if we don't?" snarled the heavily armed warrior beside the king.

"Then you die here on this road, for you may go no further with a slave in chains."

"Pah, kill the fool," commanded the warrior. Two men at arms urged their mounts forward, but were brought down by arrows before they could reach him. A dozen archers rose from the tall grasses, their horses suddenly stood as well. The archers swiftly mounted and again drew back their bows.

Tanis shifted in the saddle then pushed back his hood. Speaking in a clear voice that reached the whole Geni column, he addressed them. "Hear me people. We will allow the Geni and those who choose to travel with them to march unharmed, but the slaves remain with us. Those of you who would remain in these lands may do so, but you do so in the clear knowledge that Elves are a free people. If you choose to stay drop all weapons and move out into that field on your right.

"You men at arms, the same applies to you. If you wish to stay drop your weapons and move over to the fields. Throw aside your swords and shields, take up the plow and you are welcome in these lands. Choose now, for your time is upon you. No slave will pass further south, and neither will those who try to hold them."

With that he wheeled his horse and, followed by his dozen archers, rode away into the rising sun. A number of people left the column and headed into the open field. Many of these were folk the Elves had burned out the previous year. Those who had lived in wealth and comfort under the rule of the Geni were terrified, but made no move to join the others.

Many of the men at arms also began to throw down their weapons and ride away. These men had been forced by the Geni to drive their own families out into the winter winds to die. They had nothing for the Geni except hatred. Had the Elf asked them to revolt they probably would have. At least this way, they had a chance they might find any surviving members of their families.

Seeing this the king's brother began to shout and organize the troops to stop those leaving. It took him a while, but he managed to regain some order then the column began to move out, a full half of the warriors guarding the slaves and the rest guarding the king. That's when the Elves struck.

They poured out of the trees, riding hard at the head of the Geni army. The king shrieked in fear at the sight of the oncoming danger. As the Reavers neared, they split into two groups. They sped past the Geni and loosed a hail of arrows into the massed enemy. The king howled in pain as an arrow grazed his exposed cheek.

The men at arms gave chase, but the smaller horses were far too fast. In a short time the war horses carrying heavily armored men had tired and were slowing down. As the Geni forces became spread out they became easy targets for the faster Elves. Realizing the folly of trying to pursue the Elves, the king's brother called his men back to the road.

The Geni had started the day with two hundred mounted men and three hundred footmen. By high sun the mounted men had been reduced to half their number, many dead or badly wounded, and several had dropped weapons and ridden away to join the other deserters in the field.

During the battle that morning the Geni did not see as a small number of Elves appeared to lead the deserters back to the other side of Argar's ashes, well away from the fighting. A number of the slaves had also broken free and followed them. The Geni guards were too afraid to give chase.

When the Geni general had regained a semblance of order they began to move out once again, but again the Elves attacked. This time they were not pursued into the open fields. Seeing the men at arms wouldn't engage them they attacked the men guarding the slaves.

That sudden change in tactics startled the Geni, and they were slow to respond. By the time they realized what was happening and turned to defend the guards, fully half the remaining slaves had broken free and were being defended by mounted Elves as they fled after the deserters heading back past Argar.

With the mounted Elves committed to defending the escaped slaves they were vulnerable, and the Geni attacked again. Suddenly the air was rent by a scream of insane rage as a giant ran from the trees. Wielding a massive club, he ran right at the mounted Geni. That club swept rider after rider from his horse, their bodies crushed and broken.

Brak's sudden appearance gave Tanis the diversion he needed. As Garret led his people out into the field to defend the fleeing slaves, the Reavers were freed to renew their attack. Several riders tried to surround and bring down the giant, but it was fruitless. He simply knocked them down and ignored their blows. The few still in the saddle turned and fled, pursued by the Reavers.

As darkness began to creep over the land the Geni were down to a personal guard for the king still mounted and barely a hundred fifty foot soldiers. They huddled together in the road, still well within sight of Argar's ruins.

Morning dawned and again they faced a lone rider in the road. This one was different, lighter of build and her mount was a massive war horse. The beast pranced and snorted, spoiling for a fight, but the rider held him in check. The alarm sounded and the Geni struggled to get in the saddle.

Finally all the mounted Geni moved toward the lone figure that blocked their path. They were well within bow shot before she spoke. "You may go no further."

"And who's to stop us?" demanded king Kratec. "Who are you to command me?"

The big gray charger reared and screamed a challenge, but the rider brought him under control. She swept back her hood and faced the Geni. "I am Ariel, High Born Queen Returned. Look around you." She raised her arm and they began pouring from the trees. Elves, both mounted and afoot, thousands of them.

"Hear me, Geni. Release all your slaves to me and I will let you pass unhindered. Those others who travel with you may remain to work the farms and fields if they choose to do so. Know this people, there will be no slavery tolerated within my realm." Still no one moved within the ranks of the Geni, so she spoke again.

"Look to your left, Geni. Do you see that woman riding with a war band of Orcs? She is the Blacksmith of Fugitive, Freida who wields the god sword. If those slaves aren't moving toward freedom by the count of five she will attack you. If she does then I won't be able to stop her until every Geni is dead. Decide quickly."

"I have no fear of a blacksmith slave," roared the king's brother as he faced Freida across the field. "Come at me and meet your doom, wench."

For an answer Freida swung her leg over the saddle and landed lightly on the ground. She cast aside her cloak and tunic. As she strode toward the mounted man she swept the sword from its scabbard and spun it lightly through the air. With a bellow of challenge he spurred his horse and charged at her.

Everyone held their breath as he bore down on her. Freida easily ducked beneath his blow then seized his arm and swung herself onto the horse behind him. A lightning pass of the sword and his head fell to the ground to be followed by the body as she thrust him from the saddle and turned the horse to face the Geni.

Freida raised her fist into the air then thrust one finger toward the sky. "One." A second finger rose. "Two," said Ariel.

"Release the slaves," screamed the king. "Release the slaves, now!"

The guards who stood transfixed by the sight of the half naked Elf aboard their prince's war horse suddenly came back to life. They practically drove the slaves toward her, shouting at them to hurry. When all slaves had left the roadway to be swallowed up by the Elvish army, Ariel spoke again.

"You may leave now, Geni. Continue south to your ancient homeland. Do not leave the road, but hasten your steps southwards. My warriors will be following you to make certain you stay on the road as agreed.

"Know that all warriors who follow you are former slaves who bear no love for Geni. I caution you to give them no reason to attack. Now go."

The Geni king wasted no time obeying that command. He spurred his horse into a run and fled south, his followers doing their best to keep him in sight. Many Orcs and humans remained on the roadway. Ariel approached them. "You would remain in these lands and accept my rule?"

As one then knelt before her while Grimm snorted and pranced. "We would remain and be loyal subjects of the High Born Queen," said one Orc.

"Then I accept you. You may go where you will and do as you please. The town of Argar will begin to rebuild on the morrow. I'm certain a use can be found for any who are willing to work. I wish you well."

She turned and spoke to the man beside her in a language they could not understand. They watched as he spoke to another then that one led two hundred riders after the fleeing Geni. They soon found themselves alone on the road as the Queen led the rest of her people away. It was not yet high sun.

Freida and the Orcs joined Ariel as she slowly rode toward the ashes of Argar. "We've done it, Freida. Just as we swore to do, we set them all free."

"There's still Kress," came the reply.

"Kress has already fallen, Princess Freida," said Trelanth. "It seems I must have dropped my guard and the two mages of Kress managed to see all that passed here this day. I believe it was your dealing with the king's brother that convinced them to surrender the city."

"The king's brother? So that's who that was. He gave me a very fine horse. I think I'll keep him."

Ariel laughed with delight at that. "So, Trelanth, Kress has fallen. Tell me all."

"The overlord surrendered the slaves, my Queen, and then led the Geni and followers through the gates. They now take the road to Draton and from there south. Mexah follows with two hundred warriors to make certain they arrive.

"Lord Arlon looted the city and even now sets it ablaze. He awaits your orders, my Queen."

"How many slaves came from those gates?"

"Nearly a thousand, Lady."

"Tell him to take them to Elfhome. We'll return to Shotar and burn it down. Now, Trelanth, I have work for you and your mages."

"We're happy to serve, my Queen. What would you have of us?"

"I want a wide roadway from Argar to Fugitive, and then another to the road past Shotar that will make travel to Narthwood easier."

"It will be a great pleasure to serve, my Queen."

Ariel turned back to Freida. "My beloved sister, would you consider taking your personal guard and keeping the mages safe as they return to Fugitive?"

"It will be an honor and a pleasure, my sister. Rakka, my friend, what think you? Is it time to go home?"

"Yes, I believe it best," grinned Rakka. "Drakkat is pouting that the Geni fled without a battle. I think he needs to go home and tend to his clan." Drakkat roared with laughter at that.

Ariel then turned to Tanis. "I set you a mighty task two years ago, dear friend. You have exceeded all expectation. What would you have of me as a reward?"

"My lady Queen, it's reward enough to serve you, but, if I might, may I remain to help the good folk of Argar rebuild their town?"

"Yes, my friend, you may. Kern and the Reavers will be gone for a long time as they herd the Geni south. Choose another two hundred and remain. Inform the rest they will accompany me and the newly freed slaves as we march to Northwood. We will leave in the morning. For now, perhaps we should see to feeding our new Bornani."

"At once, my Queen. May I also keep Arlaith and Lord Julie here with me?"

"Lord Julie?"

"They arrived from Magdan, and within two days Julie had taken the headman's job, stolen my title, then organized the place better than I could have managed in a year. The girl is a wonder. With her in charge all I'll have to do is lay in the sun and grow lazy."

Ariel laughed heartily at that. "Keep whoever you need, Tanis, then have the rest ready to travel with me."

Grinning with delight, he rode away toward the people returning from the forest.

Mearith sat quietly aboard her black charger. Ariel reached out to gently grip her arm. "What is it, my heart? What troubles your thoughts?"

"The magnitude of the task before us, my delight," she replied.

"The task? Have we not done what we set out to do? Is the task not complete?" asked Ariel.

"No, my beloved, we've only just begun. Yes, we set them all free, and faster than I imagined, for I fully expected it to take many years to accomplish this."

"So what's left to do?"

"Now we must help our allies rebuild, then teach the Bornani how to live in peace and harmony with their former masters as well as with each other. There are still all the monsters and beasts the Geni set loose to deal with, Ethor is still in the mountains trying to build alliances with the Coti, there is the matter of the sea rovers to consider ..."

"Stop, Mearith, stop, you're making my head hurt. Can't we just enjoy this victory for a little while before we get mired in all the others tasks?"

Mearith smiled gently. "Yes, my delight, we can, and we should. Come, let's find a friendly campfire and see if anyone will feed us. We've destroyed the old society of these lands, tomorrow we begin to create a new one. We'll need our rest."

As darkness fell the fields were lit by campfires. The people had all come out of the forest and the work of rebuilding had already begun. Ariel had watched as Julie quietly spoke to one and then another of the people. To the queen's delight order began to evolve from the chaos of the morning.

Ariel called Arlaith and Julie to her. "Ladies. I'm quite impressed. Julie, you amaze me. You've chosen your bonded companion well, Arlaith."

"Ah, well, we haven't actually sworn the bond as yet..."

"You haven't yet sworn the bond?" Ariel was grinning and Arlaith was blushing furiously. "Why ever not?"

Julie rose to her feet, fists on hips, facing Arlaith. "Yes, about that, why haven't we sworn the bond yet?"

Blushing and sputtering helplessly, Arlaith turned to Mearith. "Lady Mearith, help me."

"Oh, it's far too late for that," grinned Mearith. "As a warrior of long experience, I'd say your best chance for survival now is to surrender."

Laughing and still blushing, Arlaith turned and pulled Julie into her arms. "Julie, my beloved cuddle buddy, will you swear the bond with me?"

"I'd love to," she replied, snuggling into Arlaith's arms. "Is that allowed? You're an Elf and I'm human. Can we actually do that?"

"Yes you can," smiled Ariel. "Now, the bond is witnessed. I believe we've all had enough of war, it's time to celebrate life."

She lifted her head and when she spoke her voice magically carried to all the people. "Hear me, good people. The war is over and now we begin to rebuild, but first we have a task. We need celebrate the sworn bond of Argar's headman and the commander of the Elvish garrison I will one day station here.

"Build up the fires, beat the drums, let us dance and sing to celebrate the union of Arlaith and Julie, those who kept the folk of Argar safe from harm."

From somewhere in the darkness a drum began and soon another joined in. A voice was raised in a song of love and joy. With a wild cry of delight Mearith swept Julie into a dance around the fire. She passed her off to Arlaith then pulled Ariel into the dance. Almost as one the Borni leaped to their feet and danced around the fires, pulling the Bornani, and others into the wild joyous celebration.

So ends the third chronicle of the Elves of Elandor. Their war of rebellion over, their freedom achieved, and the endless years of joyous renewal stretching out before them.

Don't miss out!

Visit the website below and you can sign up to receive emails whenever Prudence MacLeod publishes a new book. There's no charge and no obligation.

https://books2read.com/r/B-A-ZKBBB-JHQZC

BOOKS 2 READ

Connecting independent readers to independent writers.

Also by Prudence MacLeod

Children of the Goddess
Lady Blue
Fallen Angel
Lady Justice
Lady Shadow
Lady Seeker
Watcher and Warrior
Shadow Ascending

Children of the Wild
Immortal Tigress
Children of the Wolf
Vampire's Lair
The Hawk and the Wolf
The Oregon Incident
Race the Wind
Heir to the Throne

Elvish Chronicles
Rise of the Queen

The Road Home
A Winter Seige

Forgotten Worlds
Suvi
Echo of the Past
Survivors
Ship
Fleet
Unite
IGEN
T.E.N.

Nova series
Novan Witch
Assassin of Nova
Beyond Nova
Claimstake
Red Nova

Watch for more at https://www.prudencemacleod.com/.

Telling a story is like knitting a sweater. Start with a ball of possibilities, pull out one small thread and begin. With luck and patience you will create something quite wonderful.

About the Author

On a far off windswept island Jennifer Crandall sits with her dogs and cats creating fantastic stories for all to enjoy. She publishes as JL Crandall, Prudence MacLeod, and Jenni Leigh.

Read more at https://www.prudencemacleod.com/.